Hiding in Plain Sight
Paperback Copyright © 2021 Lorhainne Ekelund
Editor: Talia Leduc

All rights reserved.
ISBN-13 978-1989698679

Give feedback on the book at:
lorhainneeckhart@hotmail.com

Twitter: @LEckhart
Facebook: AuthorLorhainneEckhart

Printed in the U.S.A

HIDING IN PLAIN SIGHT

Billy Jo McCabe Mystery

LORHAINNE ECKHART

The Billy Jo McCabe Mystery

Nothing As It Seems
Hiding in Plain Sight
The Cold Case
The Trap
Above the Law

The social worker and the cop, an unlikely couple drawn together on a small, secluded Pacific Northwest island where nothing is as it seems. Protecting the innocent comes at a cost, and what seems to be a sleepy, quiet town is anything but.

The Social Worker

Billy Jo McCabe wants only to help children overcome their troubled lives, as she herself struggles to forget the childhood nightmare she survived. She took sociology and prelaw at the insistence of her adoptive father, Chase

McCabe, and learned how to use power tools from her adoptive mother, Rose. She loves reading in the backs of bookstores before tucking the book back on the shelf and slipping out without paying. She has a fondness for peanut butter and dill pickle sandwiches, has a three-legged cat named Harley, hates running (because that was all she did as a kid), and secretly binges on brownies and red wine on the sofa in front of her TV every Friday night.

She's never been married and has dated only twice. She visits Chase and Rose when summoned and shows up dutifully for every holiday with her family, but she has no siblings to speak of, and she feels a growing resentment for the mother who abandoned her in foster care. Despite proudly maintaining the same prickly attitude that nearly landed her behind bars as a kid, she has yet to speak up to Chase, who interferes in her life too frequently, ready to fix every problem, whether she wants him to or not.

One thing no one knows about Billy Jo is that she moved to Roche Harbor because it's the only clue she has about the last known whereabouts of the woman who abandoned her.

The Cop

Mark Friessen, son of Jed and Diana Friessen, has landed accidently in the role of small-town detective, a position in which he's going nowhere. Nearly married once, and broken-hearted three times, he's sworn he'll stay single forever, and he keeps his tattoo of a former girlfriend as a reminder that only fools fall in love. He's tall, attractive, and stubborn, and he refuses to live in the shadow of his two older brothers, Chris and Danny.

As Roche Harbor's youngest detective, he sleeps with a gun under his pillow. He has a stray dog that won't leave, and he swears that the only two food groups that exist are meat and potatoes. His favorite drink is black coffee in the morning, sugared coffee in the afternoon, and a shot of whiskey in his coffee at night to keep him warm.

****Each book in this series is a complete book, with no cliff-hangers, and can be read as a standalone. However, these books may contain references to situations from earlier books in the series. As with any long book series that focuses on specific characters, their changing relationships, and how their lives continue to unfold, you may find it more enjoyable to read the series in order of publishing, as there will be developments and changes in the relationship dynamics of the core characters.*

"No matter how much you think you want to know about something, sometimes the truth is worse."

Catlou

"This book left me an emotional mess. It provoked so many raw emotions that I found myself looking for tissues more than once while reading.

Rebmay

"Another powerful story from Ms. Eckhart! Lots of mystery and intrigue!"

Kathy, Goodreads Reviewer

Hiding in Plain Sight

A long-buried secret that was never meant to be uncovered could suddenly put a target on both Detective Mark Friessen and Billy Jo McCabe.

Twenty-five years ago, Billy Jo was born to a meth addict and spent her first few months being weaned off the drug. Labeled a difficult baby, she was bounced from foster home to foster home. Later, she was called trouble, a runner, and was accused of starting fires and stealing. She pulled a knife on one foster brother and threatened to bash in the head of another, then spent time in jail by the age of fifteen. That was before she pulled a gun at a gas station and was adopted by Chase McCabe. Her file was then sealed.

However, Billy Jo feels growing resentment for the woman responsible for her first fifteen years of hell, the one who tossed her away as if she were garbage. That has her seeking out leads as to where her real mother is, her last known whereabouts based on the sealed file she isn't technically supposed to access. But following the rules is not something Billy Jo is known for, especially not when she's playing amateur detective, asking about a woman who evidently doesn't want to be found.

Before long, Detective Mark Friessen shows up on her doorstep after someone files a complaint against her, warning her about harassing the locals. But then Billy Jo finds herself terrorized by someone determined to stop her from uncovering the truth.

Trusting anyone in her search could come at a cost, as Billy Jo soon learns that when her mother disappeared, she took with her a secret that someone doesn't want unearthed. Ultimately, her quest for answers puts a target on her that could see her killed, and that leaves Billy Jo once again forced to trust Mark, a man she will likely always be at odds with.

When Billy Jo thought of Carly Thornton, never in a million years had she pictured a white picket fence.

She parked on the street, looking out at the house, a cute two-story craftsman with teal trim and a front porch with two comfy lounge chairs, a welcoming invitation to come sit and visit. She took a second to check whether she had the right address.

This had to be a joke.

She couldn't pry her hands from where they were wrapped around her black steering wheel, the car still idling. She took in the houses on both sides of the street, the kind of homes that implied family, community, respectability, where people likely spent Saturdays barbecuing with neighbors.

This had to be the wrong Carly Thornton. But then, the trail had gone cold here after so much digging. The curiosity Billy Jo hadn't been able to shake suddenly turned into anger, which had her turning off the car, yanking on the door handle, and stepping out, unable to pull her eyes from the respectable neighborhood around her.

This was a mistake. Perhaps she had been wrong about the name. After all, Carly Thornton must have been a common name, like Jane Smith. She hesitated as soon as the thought hit her, though. After all her digging, following this cold trail, she knew that the last known location of her mother—scratch that, of the woman who'd given birth to her, was here. And how many people named Carly Jane Thornton, with the same birthdate, with a mother whose maiden name was Holloway, could be living on the island?

The records had huge gaps in time and a ton of inaccuracies, as if Carly didn't want to be found, but then, with a father like Chase McCabe, who could literally find a needle in a haystack, Billy Jo had learned from the best.

She gave her door a shove closed and left it parked on the narrow street, hearing the sounds of the morning, sprinklers running and a dog barking. She put one foot in front of the other and started walking up to the driveway. The grass was carefully manicured and green even though most of the island was facing a water shortage, and the perennials and bushes appeared well cared for.

She fisted her hands, feeling the curiosity that had driven her building in the pit of her stomach again. Wearing sandals and faded green capris, she looped her baggy purse over her shoulder and took in the car in the driveway, a silver BMW, only a few years old. Everything about the house appeared pristine, neat and tidy, nothing like what she'd expected from an addict.

The inside door was closed, and the screen door was white. Her heartbeat kicked up as she tapped on it, and it rattled. She heard footsteps, feeling her rage building, a frown pulling at her lips. Her heart thumped once, long and loud, as the door opened, and she stared into blue eyes, dark hair, and a smile she hadn't expected.

"Hello. Can I help you?"

It was her voice, soft. She didn't appear that old, and she wasn't much taller than Billy Jo, about five foot two. She pushed open the screen, and Billy Jo glimpsed inside the house behind her, seeing gleaming hardwood and nice furnishings, hearing voices and footsteps from what she thought was the kitchen.

"I'm looking for Carly Thornton. My name is Billy Jo McCabe. I hope this doesn't sound totally strange, but the searches I've done show that this house is where she lives."

The woman's smile suddenly faltered, and she didn't know what to make of her expression.

"Are you Carly?" Billy Jo finally asked.

"You have the wrong house," the woman said. "I've never heard of Carly Thornton. Who are you, anyway—a bill collector, a solicitor? The sign clearly says we don't accept any here." She pointed to a sign by the door, *No soliciting*.

So she didn't like strange people showing up. Billy Jo knew well when someone was uncomfortable, though. She could tell from the tension in her expression.

"Carly, who's at the door?" a man called out.

Billy Jo heard his footsteps before he appeared behind the woman. About her dad's age, he had dark hair and hazel eyes, and he smiled, holding a mug of coffee. His hand rested on the woman's shoulder.

"Oh, just someone who's lost and looking for directions, is all," the woman said. "Can you see that the girls finish breakfast and get ready for school? We're running late already."

Billy Jo stood in silence, watching. The man was tall, solidly built, wearing blue jeans, a golf shirt, and a wedding ring. He looked over to her and back to the woman, and the two exchanged the kind of look a husband and wife shared. "Don't be long, then," he said. "You said you had to leave earlier for the school meeting, and don't forget we have the Davidson fundraiser tonight."

Then he stepped away from the door, and the woman angled her head to him and gave him a smile. As he walked away, though, and she dragged her gaze back to Billy Jo, her face was filled with the kind of unfriendliness she hadn't seen in a long time.

"So you are Carly?" Billy Jo said, the heaviness inside her now building into a sick feeling.

"Look, I don't know who you are or what you want, but I asked nicely," the woman said. "Please go away. I already told you that you have the wrong house." She actually stepped out and pulled the inside door closed quietly behind her, holding the screen so it wouldn't slap closed.

Secrets and lies. She knew when someone was holding out on her. Billy Jo had to step back, really taking in this woman, who was of the same height and build as her. Her hair reached her shoulders, and she was dressed casually, much like Billy Jo. The panic and something else in her expression said she didn't want Billy Jo asking about Carly Thornton.

"I don't know why you're pretending you're not her," Billy Jo said. "By your reaction, only a fool would miss that you're hiding something. Let me tell you that finding you wasn't easy. The trail was hidden and cold, and someone went to a lot of trouble to make it that way. I didn't have a clue what I was going to say to you, but here it is. I was born twenty-five years ago in a small Nevada town, on June 15th, to a meth addict. I spent my first few months being weaned off the drug. As a baby, I was difficult to care for, and I was in and out of the ER, being bounced around from foster home to foster home. I think, by your face, your expression, your reaction to me, that you're my mother. I've been looking for you for a really long time. But what I can't understand is this picture-perfect life you have now, or how you just abandoned me to the hell I lived through for fifteen years until I was finally adopted by my parents…"

"Look," the woman said. "This Carly Thornton you say you're looking for is not me. She doesn't exist. I'm sorry for what you've been through, and it sounds horrible, but that's not on me. I would appreciate you not coming back here again. Please leave. I wish you the best of luck finding this woman, but she's not me. Now, if you don't mind, I need to get back to my family and get my girls ready for school." She was still holding the door, and the expression on her face was guarded.

"I don't know what you're hiding or why you want to pretend this isn't you, but I think I deserve some answers," Billy Jo said. "I have a right. No, I demand—"

"You have no right to anything," the woman said, cutting her off quite sharply. She took a step toward her, letting the screen door close and forcing Billy Jo back closer to the steps. Her voice was low and quiet. "I'm going to ask you just one more time: Please leave, please. I have a good life here, a husband, children. You said you were adopted, you have a mother and father? Good, because they're your family. It sounds to me as if you're looking to dig up a problem that should stay buried. Don't bring this to my doorstep, trying to search for answers down memory lane. It's not going to happen." She reached for the screen door and pulled it open, then for the knob of the closed inside door.

"Wait, please," Billy Jo said. She could feel this slipping away, this opportunity to look the woman she hated in the eye, but this was nothing like what she'd expected. "I know you're her. I just want some answers, please."

"Carly Thornton no longer exists. I'm sorry for whatever happened to you, but by the looks of it, you appear to be doing fine. As you said, you have a family who adopted you. That was a long time ago. Please go away—and don't come back. Please." There was nothing friendly in her tone, and the way she looked at Billy Jo with such anger, hate, and fear tore open that giant wound inside her that had never really healed.

Billy Jo put her hands on the screen door before the woman could close it, but the woman still moved to open the inside door. "Look, I just want some questions answered. I'll come back another time so we can talk, but I think I deserve that much."

All the woman did was step back inside and shake her head, then said in a low voice, "Please go, please, and don't come back. You're entitled to nothing."

Then the door closed in her face.

Billy Jo looked over to the living room window as she turned to take a step down. Two girls, maybe eight and ten, had parted the blinds and were looking out before the woman pulled them away.

She stepped down the two steps from the porch, taking in this perfection, the perfect life this woman now had. So that was Carly Thornton, who was nothing like the meth-addicted woman who'd abandoned her.

Instead of resolving anything, the meeting had left rage bubbling up inside her. Carly had dumped her and had been responsible for her childhood of hell, and now she got a free pass to have a great life?

As she walked back to her car, looking once more at the perfect house, the perfect yard, and the image of a perfect family, she felt like garbage, unwanted. She knew there was no way this woman was getting a pass.

No, she'd keep coming back, and she'd figure out a way to get the answers she wanted, the answers she deserved. There was no way she was going to let herself be a dirty little secret Carly was trying to forget. Billy Jo was going to make damned sure her birth mother told her everything.

Chapter 2

"So I see you do know how to make coffee," Carmen Zarco said, dressed in the brown deputy uniform she always wore. Her dark hair was pulled back in a ponytail, and she was holding an empty mug. Her dark eyes were unsmiling, but then, Mark didn't think she ever smiled.

"Of course I know how to make coffee," he replied as he reached for the carafe, which was still filling, and held it up to pour her a mug and then himself.

Carmen set her mug down, reached for a packet of sugar and powdered creamer, and stirred them both in using one of the clean spoons Gail kept organized at the coffee station. She said nothing else.

Carmen wasn't known for talking. Maybe that was why she and Mark got along so well, but then, what did he know about a woman who held her cards close to her chest? Not much.

"So what's on the island agenda for today?" he said. "Seems pretty quiet." He never really knew what Carmen was up to when she did her rounds, driving through Roche Harbor, talking to people. She didn't share much.

She flicked her gaze up to him after dropping her spoon in the sink, then lifted the steaming coffee, blew on it, and took a swallow. She made a face as if it were too hot. "You trying to jinx it? Just the same old. I'll head out for rounds in a minute after I finish all the paperwork, but it seems the summer craziness is finally slowing down, with the return to school. There's still the usual fall tourists, with parties and noise complaints, public intoxication, camping in the park, general indecency…

"Oh, and my favorite last night was the million-dollar yacht now half underwater in the public dock because the owner figured drinking and driving laws didn't apply to boats or him. Thankfully, that falls on the coast guard and not on me. Let them deal with the asshole and his fancy lawyer, who's trying to spin some technical bullshit about how the dock doesn't meet current federal guidelines, which require a specific allowance from shore." She gestured to his face. "My response exactly. Seriously, these rich assholes show up here and figure they can do anything they want. Then their shithead lawyers spin it so nothing is their fault. Trying to pin it on a dock, really? And what pisses me off is that he'll get away with it."

"Hmm, glad I wasn't there," Mark said. He knew Carmen hated calls like that. Usually, the chief handled anything that required hand-holding and schmoozing.

He heard the door and turned to see a tall, dark-haired man, casually dressed The man looked over to Gail, the chief's wife, who was just packing up her bag on her pristinely neat desk.

"Hey, Jim, great to see you," Gail said. "What brings you down here?"

Apparently, they knew each other. Mark turned back to

Carmen, who was staring over at the man, watching him the same way she watched everyone, as if he were suspicious and up to something. Yeah, trust issues ran deep here.

"You talk to the chief this morning?" Mark said. If Gail was leaving, that generally meant the chief was on his way in.

"Nope, but I'm sure we will soon," Carmen said. "Guess I'd better get that report filed before he demands it."

As she walked over to her desk, not far from his in the bullpen, also neat and tidy, the station door opened to reveal Chief Tolly Shepard, a big man in a ballcap and sunglasses. His mustache appeared freshly trimmed, and he wore khakis and a golf shirt.

"Well, this is a surprise, Jim," the chief said. "Didn't know you were coming down. You working an angle for another golf game, trying to whoop my ass again?" He shook the man's hand and patted his arm. So they were golf buddies.

"Yeah, well, I'll win every time," Jim said. "There was no angle there. The one and only time you won was an off day. Just remember that! But I'm here on another matter, just something I need you to check into. An issue showed up on my doorstep this morning, and I'm hoping you can steer it away or make sure it doesn't happen again."

Mark wondered what the issue was.

The chief gestured Jim into his office. "You bet," he said. "Come on and fill me in, and I'll do what I can."

He watched as they strode into his office, still talking in a friendly back and forth, and closed the door. The chief knew a lot of people on the island and was friends with many. He did the schmoozing thing well.

An incident…maybe a theft? The chief's friends didn't

call 911. They simply dropped in or called the chief, and the chief would handle it. That, or it would suddenly become Mark's top priority, to be handled the way the chief expected.

"Okay, kids, I'm off," Gail said. "Don't go making a mess of anything. Mark, I expect you to turn off the coffee pot when you're done. I'm not coming in to clean up after you anymore. Wash your own mugs out. Tidy up. Remember, I'm not your maid or your mother."

Carmen only gave a wave to Gail, then kept on typing as the older woman walked out. Mark had noticed the passing of husband and wife, the silence, the way Gail and the chief never worked together.

He heard the chief's door open. "Hey, Mark, come in here a second," he called out.

There it was. Whatever the problem, it was now being handed over to him. He looked over to his boss, who was unsmiling, before putting his coffee mug on his desk and striding over.

"Jim, this is my detective, Mark Friessen," the chief said. "Mark, this is a good friend of mine, Jim Jackson. He says a woman showed up at his door this morning, and he's a little concerned. Apparently, she upset his wife. Can you describe her again? Short, brown hair, freckles…"

Mark found himself wondering what this was. He dragged his gaze from the chief to Jim, who was about his height, solidly built, and gestured toward them both. "And what did the woman do, exactly?"

There was a second of silence, during which he realized he wasn't supposed to have asked that.

"She upset his wife," the chief said.

Mark hadn't known that was a crime, and he wondered whether his expression and the rough laugh he let out would earn him any points. "Sorry, I'm missing something," he said. "I need a little more than that your wife is upset. Did the woman issue a threat of bodily harm, or did your wife feel as if she were being threatened in any way? Was there damage to your property or something?"

Jim suddenly seemed awkward, on edge, at the realization that Mark wasn't falling in line with his way of thinking. He could see the chief was expecting him to handle this, which was not something he appreciated.

"Seriously, Chief, unless I'm missing something here, someone showing up on your doorstep and upsetting your wife isn't exactly a crime…"

"But someone pretending to be lost only to work some scam or agenda is a problem," Jim said. "The visitor was unwanted. A friendly warning needs to be issued to her to stay away and not show up on our doorstep again, as she was trespassing. I have rights regarding who's on my property. Give her a warning and bar her from setting foot there again. I don't want my wife feeling cornered. She said the woman was a nuisance, working some angle on the locals, but I think it was more than that. I've never seen my wife so upset, so rattled. She tried to dismiss it when I asked her, just said not to worry about it, but I would like you to find her and warn her off. Make it official or not, but I don't want her showing up on my doorstep again. If she does, she won't be able to corner my wife next time."

From the way the chief nodded, Mark could feel his next order coming. "Mark, you find this lady and have a talk with her about not bothering the Jacksons again. If she doesn't take the friendly warning, then issue her a trespassing ticket."

He realized the chief was serious, but he was still lost. Working what angle? Specifics were required. "Okay, fine, but who is she? You have a name, something…?"

Jim just shook his head. "No name. She appeared to be

in her mid-twenties, with shoulder-length brown hair, dressed neat and tidy, so not some homeless transient. She drove away in a gray Corolla, and I did get a partial plate."

The man really had been watching. As Mark stared at him, though, he already knew who it was. He slid his gaze over to the chief and said, "Can I have a word with you for a second?" before opening the door and stepping out of the office.

The chief hesitated, then let out one of those sighs that meant he wasn't happy about something. "Don't you worry, Jim. I'll see to it that this is taken care of and she doesn't show up again. I'll be right back," he said. Then he followed Mark over to the coffee station, just enough out of the way.

"That sounds like Billy Jo McCabe," Mark said. "You know, the social worker here? You want me to track her down and issue her a warning? If she showed up on their doorstep, maybe there's an issue we don't know about, some complaint. Do they have kids?"

The chief stared long and hard at him, one of the things he could do well. "They have two girls, but they're fine parents, Jim and Carly. If Ms. McCabe is sniffing around, it's because of some bogus claim, so I want you to shut it down. Then you have a chat with her, find out what she was doing, and warn her off. Jim and Carly are good people. She's got no business nosing around there. See to it she understands that."

Then the chief walked away, back into his office, and Mark watched through the glass as he said something to Jim, shook his hand, and laughed.

Mark realized Carmen was looking his way. Her expression, though never amused, seemed more guarded than usual, maybe even a little pissed. But she shook her head and said nothing. He wished she'd just say whatever dark thoughts she'd been thinking, as she clearly knew something he didn't.

He started over to his desk, lifted his coffee, and reached for his cell phone to thumb through his contacts until he found Billy Jo and called her. He listened to the ring, hating this part of the job. It went right to voicemail.

"You've reached Billy Jo McCabe. I can't take your call. Leave your name and number, and I'll call you back."

He shook his head and took in Carmen, who was watching him while pretending to work. "Hey, Billy Jo," he said. "It's Detective Friessen. A bit of an issue has just come to my attention, and I need to speak with you about it, so call me back." Then he disconnected and pocketed his phone.

Carmen was holding a file, likely her finished report, as she stood up.

"So how often does this happen?" he said. He knew he didn't have to elaborate, because her expression said she understood.

"You mean doing something for the chief's friends that you wouldn't do for someone else?" she said, cutting right to it without really answering him. She raised a brow and didn't look over to the chief in his office. Just then, the door opened and Jim and the chief walked out.

"Again, don't worry, Jim. My detective will handle it," the chief said. "I look forward to seeing you and Carly tonight at that shindig."

Jim stopped in front of Mark. "You'll handle this today, Detective," he said, not a question. Apparently, the man thought he could give him his marching orders.

"I know how to do my job. Good day, Mr. Jackson," was all Mark said.

Jim glanced back to the chief. "Tolly, you'll follow this

up?" he said. There it was, cutting him off at the knees, going over his head. He hated this puppet shit.

"Don't you worry, Jim," the chief said. "My detective is good at what he does."

Jim evidently took that as his answer, as he started out of the office and pulled the door closed behind him. Mark realized Carmen was nowhere to be seen now, likely in back. How had she managed to slip out so quietly? The chief gave him a long, lingering look.

"What?" Mark said. "Seriously, Chief, what is this? You have no idea what's going on. If there's an official investigation into a child welfare issue, I can't interfere, and you know that. What is this? A friend of yours walks in and says someone's bothering him, and I'm to shut it down, make this person go away? Do you think if someone else had walked in, you'd still be all over it? This really isn't a good use of my time. Abuse of power is kind of what comes to mind."

"Are you finished?" the chief said. He had a way of handling things that Mark would never understand.

Mark reached for his keys in his pocket and pulled them out, feeling the bite in the chief's tone. There was a time to push, and then there were times when pushing would have him looking for another job.

"I'll go find Billy Jo," Mark said. "If it's her, I'll find out what's what. But you may want to ask yourself, if she showed up there, whether something may be going on with your friends, or maybe just the wife. Everyone has secrets, Chief."

His boss just pointed to the door and said, "Go handle it," then walked away.

All Mark could think was that there was a puzzle here. Secrets, lies… What exactly was going on with Jim Jackson and his wife? If it had been Billy Jo at the door, what was the real story?

He'd find out and then decide how to handle it. Just maybe, this would be the final straw, and he'd have to find himself another job someplace else.

Chapter 3

Billy Jo had just sent off an email to her boss with a finished report on her meeting with a prospective foster parent. Now, she took in the BMW she was parked beside in the half-full elementary school lot. The sprinklers were spraying water back and forth over the lawn, the kids were all inside, and Billy Jo knew Carly Thornton was there.

Detective Friessen had called her and left a message. What about, she had no clue, and right now, he was the last person she wanted to speak to. Dealing with his arrogance took a great deal of patience, digging deep to a part of herself that she didn't have the energy to find at the moment. Whatever his issue right now, the only thing she wanted was to corner this woman, who had made her feel as if she were somehow responsible for what had happened to her as a baby, an innocent baby.

She'd never been able to let go of that feeling of being unwanted.

She gave her head a shake and took in the pristine BMW again. Carly Thornton had been a mystery to her for so long, someone she was determined to find, and she was now more convinced than ever that she had stood on the right doorstep that morning, looking into the face of the right person.

She knew when someone was lying or hiding something—because in her business, someone always was. She tapped the steering wheel, considering. She'd sat for an hour, typing her report on her laptop while she waited for Carly to walk out of the school. She had two little girls, and Billy Jo couldn't help thinking that meant she had siblings, two sisters. What could that mean?

Her cell phone rang again. She reached for it and saw the detective's name, then sighed and pressed the green answer button. "What do you want?"

"Where are you right now?"

She stared at the school from her parked car, hearing a bell as the sprinklers shut off. The doors opened and kids spilled out to the schoolyard, but Carly still hadn't come out. How long would she have to wait?

"What can I do for you, Detective?" she replied. She wasn't about to answer him or explain anything about what she was doing. This was all her business, no one else's.

"Well, an issue has come up, and I need to speak with you."

"You know, I'm kind of in the middle of something, so if this can wait…"

"It can't wait." He cut her off quite sharply. "Tell me whatever you're in the middle of has nothing to do with Carly Jackson."

The way he said it made her pull her gaze from the school. He had her full attention now.

"Excuse me?" she started, suddenly at a loss for words.

"You paid a visit this morning to the Jacksons."

So Carly Thornton was now Carly Jackson.

"How would you know that?" she said. Her heart was hammering, and her palms were sweating. As she held the phone, she had to remind herself to breathe. She looked out the windshield, seeing kids and staff.

"So that was you," Mark said. "The way he described you, I thought for sure it was. Now I know. Listen, we need to talk. Where are you?"

There was something about the demand in his voice. She could tell he wasn't taking no for an answer.

"Because right now," he continued, "I'm outside your place, knocking on your door, and all I see is a three-legged cat staring back at me. You haven't gone in to work yet, I know that, so again, where are you?"

"I'm at the elementary school, in the parking lot, waiting for someone."

"I'm on my way. Don't go anywhere," he said, then hung up.

She rested the phone back in her bag on the passenger seat, seeing teachers out on the grounds, a few looking her way. Then she spotted Carly walking out of the school with another woman, talking, dressed casually, the same as that morning. Did she work there?

Billy Jo slid her laptop back in its bag on the floor of the passenger side and stepped out. She couldn't explain the ache that had come out of nowhere, seeing how good Carly looked. This was the person she'd had in the back of her mind forever.

She closed the door and took a step, but a black Jeep drove in and swung around in front of her vehicle. Mark. He stopped behind her and stepped out, dressed as he always was in faded blue jeans, a jean jacket, and cowboy boots. His deep red hair was short and appeared freshly cut, and he didn't pull off his sunglasses as he gave his door a shove closed and walked over to her. He looked past her and then right at her, angling his head.

"What, exactly, are you doing?" he said, stopping right in front of her. There was just something about him that made her suspect they would always be butting heads.

"You know, Mark, I don't go around questioning what you're doing, how you're handling an investigation, or how you act as a cop. That would be overstepping, inappropriate…"

"So you're investigating an issue. Is that what this is? Are you investigating the Jacksons, or what is this?"

She said nothing.

He let out a rough laugh. "Okay, so you don't want to answer. Seriously, Billy Jo, what the hell is going on here? Are you or are you not officially investigating the Jacksons? Are you following up on a complaint regarding their girls? Because I have to tell you that the chief is on my ass about this."

There was something about the way he said it. She could feel the rug about to be yanked out from beneath her feet.

"This is more personal," she said.

He angled his head again, then lifted his sunglasses and rested them on top of his red hair, really looking at her. "So this isn't official? Don't blow me off. I can see you don't want to answer, but you evidently stepped into something when you showed up on the Jacksons' doorstep."

She pulled her tongue over her teeth, because showing her cards was something she never did. "Let me guess: Carly filed a complaint against me."

He pulled back and knit his brow. "No, not Carly. It was her husband, Jim Jackson—who, by the way, is friends with the chief. He showed up this morning, making noise about a woman showing up on their doorstep and harassing his wife. As soon as he described her, I knew it was you, but I was hoping it wasn't, and I'm pretty sure the chief does, as well."

So Carly had a husband, Jim, and kids, and a nice house, and she was friends with the chief. She'd really stepped into it, but now she was more determined than ever, because she'd bet her bottom dollar Carly was lying about everything to her new family and friends, too.

"Okay, so it was me," Billy Jo said. "What, are you here to warn me off? Because I have to tell you, it's not going to work." She pulled her arms across her chest and took in the surprise in his expression.

He stepped back, brushed his hands over his jean jacket, and rested them on his hips. "Billy Jo, this isn't a game. You can't go showing up on the Jacksons' doorstep and harassing them. What's going on with them? If this isn't something from the DCFS, then it's personal, so what is it?" He gestured toward her.

She worked her mouth, but there was no way she was telling anyone the reason she was really there. She shook her head.

"Unbelievable. Damn it, why are you so difficult?" he snapped. She had suspected he would be quite volatile when pushed, but she'd never received this from him before. "Look, Billy Jo, I don't know what your issue is with this woman, but you can't harass the Jacksons. There are people you just can't do this with."

"You mean because they're friends of the chief," she said. "Let me guess: You were ordered to make sure I never show up on their doorstep, never talk to Carly…"

"They don't want to be bothered. They want to be left alone, and that is very much their right." He was so direct, cutting her off, and she didn't miss the warning in his expression. "And if you're confused on the law, if you continue bothering them, Jim Jackson wants you issued a trespass ticket. This is a warning, but if you show up again, he'll likely be demanding your arrest. The chief is going to side with his friend, not you, so whatever this is, stop it now."

He lifted his gaze, looking past her, and narrowed his eyes. She found herself turning to see what he was looking at, and there was Carly, staring at her with a look of pure alarm.

"Who is that?" Mark asked.

Billy Jo lifted her hand to Carly, who was now digging into each step, walking their way. "That would be Carly Jackson. So tell me, Mark, is this where you arrest me? Because I heard you. I got your warning. You know, what really gets me is how police resources seem to be inappropriately allocated here."

As she took a step over to Carly, she felt Mark's hand on her arm, pulling her back. She stared at it and lifted her gaze to him, and all he did was shake his head.

"No, Billy Jo, you listen to me. You're not talking to her. I'm going to ask you one more time to get in your car, drive out of here, and not come back again."

"Or what, Mark, you'll arrest me?"

He looked at her, really looked at her. "Don't push me, Billy Jo, because this isn't the kind of thing you can mess around with, not with me."

Chapter 4

Carly Jackson was really digging into each step as she headed right toward Billy Jo, wearing flats, dark capris, and a striped blouse. Despite all the kids in the background, Mark knew when a woman was angry. The energy seemed to explode between them. Everything about her gave him a feeling the confrontation wasn't going to be peaceful.

"Why are you here?" Carly said, hurling the angry accusation at Billy Jo. "Are you following me?"

The little spitfire beside him went to close the gap, but his feet were already moving to get between them before it went sideways.

"I have questions I need answered," Billy Jo said. "You have kids, I see, girls. I will get my answers, one way or the other."

"You are following me," Carly said. "Look, you can't be here. I have a good life. I'm a teacher."

"Hey, enough, already," Mark said. "What's going on here?" He moved between the women and put his hand up to block Billy Jo, who he knew wouldn't back down. De-escalation was the only thing he could think of as he felt both their eyes on him.

"This is personal," was all Billy Jo said to him. As she pulled her gaze from Carly, the look she gave him said she couldn't be reasoned with.

"Okay, you're not doing this here," he said. "Both of you, take a look around. There are kids here. This is a school. Who are you, anyway?" He looked right at Carly, dark hair, blue eyes. Something about her seemed familiar.

She pulled her arms across her chest, nodded, and glanced up at him. "Carly Jackson. I'm a teacher here, and this woman is harassing me. She showed up this morning on my doorstep—"

"And you didn't answer me," Billy Jo said. "You tell me to go away, yet you owe me."

He didn't know which woman to look at, to address. When his cell phone started ringing, he pulled it from his pocket and saw the chief's name. Of course, someone had seen the scene and had likely already called him. "Shit," he said under his breath, then hit decline, though he wouldn't get away with that for long.

"Billy Jo, what are you doing?" he said. "What does she owe you?" He was really hoping this was about a formal DCFS complaint.

"I said it's personal," she replied. She lifted her eyes to him again, and he saw she wasn't giving him anything, so he dragged his gaze back over to Carly Jackson. The two appeared ready to go head to head in a cat fight he didn't want on his hands.

"I asked you a question," he said matter of factly. "What is this about? Ms. Jackson, what do you owe her? What did you do?"

Carly said nothing for a moment, pulling her gaze from Billy Jo. She was a short woman, the same height and build as her, and she had to look up at him. "She's right that this is personal, but she has the wrong person," she said. She turned back to Billy Jo. "I'm not your mother."

"Wait, what?" Mark said, doing a doubletake, looking from one woman to the other. He knew he needed to end this now. He turned to Billy Jo, who seemed to be looking past Carly. "Mother? You said you were adopted, in foster care?"

"Carly, what's going on here?" said a short man approaching them. He was balding and round in the middle, wearing beige dress pants and a white shirt. "Are you all right?"

Mark pulled his jacket back to show his badge to the man as he stopped right behind Carly.

"Tony, it's fine, sorry," Carly said. "It's just a personal matter, no problem. Listen, I'll be right in."

Mark said nothing, only nodded to the man, who he figured had to be the school principal or something.

"I called the chief already," Tony said, as if he didn't believe her. "It looked like you were upset. I didn't know the police were already here." Then he just gestured toward her and said, "Recess is almost over. Do you mind taking this somewhere else?"

Carly only nodded and then offered a smile to him. "Absolutely, I'll be right in," she said.

Tony simply nodded and walked away.

Mark's phone rang. As he pulled it from his pocket and saw the chief's name, he knew he couldn't decline it again. "Yeah, look," he answered. "I'm talking to Billy Jo right now——"

"Why did I just get a call from the principal?" the chief said. "He said there appeared to be an altercation between one of his teachers, Carly Jackson, and someone harassing her. Is it Ms. McCabe? We just discussed this less than an hour ago."

Mark could feel the bite in his words. "I'm shutting it down now," he said. "It's handled."

"See that it is, and see that Ms. McCabe doesn't bother Jim's wife again. Do I make myself clear?"

"Crystal," Mark said, then heard the click as the chief hung up on him. He turned back to the two women, whose voices were low, and gestured between them.

"Look," Billy Jo said. "You keep denying that you're Carly Thornton, and you covered your tracks well. It took a lot of digging to find you, but I did. I have questions, a right to know what you did to me…"

"I did nothing to you. And by the looks of it, it appears you have a great life. I have a life here, too, a husband, kids, a career. I do not want this on my doorstep."

"Billy Jo, you can't do this here. You have to go," Mark cut in.

She only lifted her blue eyes to him. They were filled with stubbornness. She just wasn't about to be reasoned with. But she finally nodded and said, "You're right. Outside a school isn't appropriate, with everyone watching —unless you want me to start telling everyone that you, my mother, were a meth addict who abandoned me…"

"Stop!" Carly hissed. "What do you want?"

This was going from bad to worse.

"I want answers to my questions, no lies, and then you can go back to your perfect life."

He knew he needed to get Billy Jo out of there, but he couldn't believe Carly Jackson could possibly be who Billy Jo thought she was. The way she was staring at her, he could feel the secrets and lies that lingered between them. Carly was considering something, but just then, a white

Range Rover pulled into the parking lot, headed right their way.

Carly stiffened and lifted her hand. "Okay, you have to go now. That's my husband," she said.

He heard the vehicle idling. Then the car door opened to reveal Jim, the man he'd received marching orders from less than an hour earlier.

"I already told you I'm not this woman," Carly said. "Now, I'm sorry, but you're going to have to leave. I won't be threatened or harassed." She lifted her gaze up to Mark, then walked around Billy Jo, over to Jim. "What are you doing here?" she said as he slid his arm around her.

Jim took in Mark and then dragged his gaze to Billy Jo, and Mark could see the simmer there, the edge of a man who wouldn't be pushed. "What is she doing here?" he said. "What do you want? Detective, we had a discussion, and I was clear that I want this woman to stop harassing my wife."

"Jim, it's fine," Carly said. "It's just a misunderstanding, is all. Look, you didn't have to come running down here."

Jim only nodded to his wife. Mark suspected this could turn ugly quick. But at the same time, he knew when someone was hiding something.

"Of course I did," Jim said. "Tony called from the school, and I told him to call the chief. I saw how upset you were this morning. Detective, I want this woman charged. You said this would be handled. Who are you, anyway, and what do you want with my wife?"

Jim wasn't going to walk away. Answers needed to be given, but he heard a bell, and the kids were starting to go back into the school. This wasn't the place to be having this kind of discussion. He should say something. Billy Jo was considering the situation, and he could see what looked like fear in Carly's expression.

Billy Jo shrugged. "Carly Thornton is your wife?" she said.

Mark wanted to swear, but he also wanted to know more.

Jim shrugged. "Her maiden name is Thornton. What is this about?"

Carly stared long and hard at Billy Jo before saying, "I knew her mother. I wasn't sure at first. She just has some questions. Isn't that right, Billy Jo?"

The way Jim was watching her, her hand on his chest, Mark could see he was having trouble with this.

"We were just about to make arrangements to meet and talk," Carly said before looking right at Billy Jo. "Isn't that right?"

He wondered whether Billy Jo would agree, by how tight her mouth seemed, but then she nodded. "That's right," she said, gesturing toward her. "We were just checking our calendars. After school today, we'll meet, catch up, talk…"

"You can't today," Jim said. "Remember, we have the charity event at the golf club."

Carly made a face and touched her forehead. "Right, sorry. I forgot about that. It will have to be another time."

"Well, how about dinner tomorrow at our house?" Jim said. "She can come over and—"

"Dinner tomorrow at your house sounds great," Billy Jo cut in.

Mark found himself staring between them, wondering how Carly would manage to talk her way out of that.

All she did was nod. "Sure. Listen, you need to go. I have to get back in," she said.

Carly kissed her husband, who walked away and

climbed back into his Range Rover, and Mark didn't have a clue what to ask, what to say. She turned back to Billy Jo, then lifted her gaze to him, uncomfortable, cornered.

"Look, my husband may have invited you for dinner, but I don't want you to come," she said. "You want answers? Fine. I'll meet you after school at the coffee house. I'll answer your questions. Then I don't want you to bother me again. Detective, I'd appreciate your discretion about this." She gestured to him.

He could see how rattled she was. "I'm just trying to keep the peace," he said

She nodded and walked away, hurrying back toward the school. The Range Rover gave a quick honk of a goodbye.

Mark stared down at Billy Jo, wondering about the little bomb that had been deployed. "Well, that was interesting. How about you start at the beginning and fill me in on everything?"

She narrowed her eyes as if telling him where to go. Then she shrugged. "This is personal, Detective. Are you about to charge me or something? As you heard, this was nothing but a friendly discussion, a personal matter. Her husband over-reacted and called your chief, so from my end, it appears as if you're wasting your time here. You heard her. She's meeting me after school…"

"She's your mother, who doesn't want to be found," he cut in, stepping closer.

There it was, that pull at her lips that seemed like a smile but wasn't. "Well, that's the thing. It's too late. I've found her. She can't un-ring this bell. So, if that's all, have a great day." She actually took a step to her car, dismissive, not to be convinced of anything.

"No, that's not all, Billy Jo. You don't want to give me a

straight answer. She was a meth addict who abandoned you? I guess I'd be pretty pissed, too."

"Detective, as you said, you have a mother and father who love you. You've never known the kinds of things I have, being tossed away like garbage." She had a sharp tongue, direct.

"Point taken, but here's your warning: You meet with her, no shenanigans, and then you leave her be. Although you may feel you have the right to answers, she also has the right to live in peace and not be harassed. So make sure this is as far as it goes. The Jacksons are friends of the chief. If Carly has the kind of past you're alluding to, I guarantee you her husband doesn't know. So be sure this is just about getting answers and not about exacting some sort of revenge, destroying her life."

She pulled at her door and then let out a breath as she looked up to him. "Again, Detective, have a great day. This is my business."

She slid into her car, pulled the door closed, and started it. Then she shoved on her sunglasses, waiting for him to move his Jeep, which was parked right behind her. All he could see was a woman who wasn't concerned with fitting into this community, making peace and keeping this secret. No, he was absolutely, one hundred percent positive that this was only the beginning of something that could turn into a shitstorm.

Chapter 5

"Can I get you another coffee?"

Billy Jo, who had been typing on her laptop, answering emails, and waiting for Carly Thornton to arrive, looked up to the young woman standing beside her table. She had long blond hair in a high ponytail, slender, tall, and cute. After one latte and then a regular coffee, Billy Jo was sweating from the caffeine high.

"No, actually, could I just get a glass of water?" she replied. "Hey, is school out here at three thirty?"

She wondered whether she had the time wrong, but then, knowing how understaffed schools were, she suspected the teachers usually left later than the kids.

"The elementary school is out at three twenty," the waitress said. "You have kids there? You must be new to the island. I don't recognize you." She had a really nice smile, but she was far too interested in Billy Jo's business.

She took in the dark wood tables in the small coffee house, a few occupied. She had sat beside the window so she could see who was coming and going. "No, I have no kids. I moved here not long ago."

The clock on the wall was approaching five, and she had a sinking feeling in her stomach, knowing Carly wasn't going to show.

"Welcome to the community," the waitress said. "I'll get you your water and be right back."

Billy Jo closed up her laptop just as she spotted the door opening. The bell rang, and she sat up straighter, taking in the tall, rugged redhead that filled the doorway. Detective Mark Friessen stepped inside, his sunglasses resting on top of his head.

"Hey, Mark, you want your usual?" the blonde called out to him from behind the counter.

He tossed her an easy smile. "Sure, thanks, Sybil."

Billy Jo couldn't pull her gaze from him. The moment he saw her, he looked around as if tracking everyone in the place, then strode to her, slow and with purpose. She knew he had something on his mind. She made herself look away, then tucked her laptop into her bag on the chair beside her.

He stopped at her small table and rested his hands on the back of the empty chair across from her with that direct look of his, those vibrant blue eyes that she didn't want in her business. "So you're still here. You meet Carly Jackson?"

She should've said yes and then told him to go away, mind his own business. She couldn't have explained to anyone how the idea of Mark knowing even a little bit of her tainted background bothered her. The fact was that Carly had lied to her again.

She knew he was still waiting as the waitress appeared with her water and Mark's coffee in a go mug.

"Thanks, Sybil." He pulled a five from his pocket and handed it to her.

"Anytime, Mark," Sybil replied, and Billy Jo didn't miss the extra sway in her step as she walked away.

Mark was giving all his attention to her. The way he looked at her with that shrewdness, she knew his appearance at the coffee house wasn't a coincidence. "Well, where is she?" he said. "You talk? You get your answers? Because I have to tell you, the chief is chomping at the bit and is ready to take a bite out of my ass if I don't rein you in."

She didn't much appreciate the way he spoke about her. "Well, you'll be happy to know she didn't show."

He said nothing at first, just glanced away, shook his head, and then pulled out the chair across from her. He sat down as if he'd been invited. "I didn't see that coming, but I guess it's expected. She's really your mother?" He lifted the takeout lid from his coffee and took a swallow before flicking those brilliant blue eyes her way again. The question was there. Yeah, he was more than curious.

"And if she is?" she replied. "Again, this is personal, and I'd rather not have you knowing anything about my business." Even she could hear how snippy she'd sounded.

What did he do but laugh as he leaned forward on the table? "I think we're way past that," he said, "considering I've basically got the chief on my back to keep you off the Jacksons. You're stepping on toes again, Billy Jo, but I have a feeling that's all you know how to do. So she's your mother. Is this the one who abandoned you to foster care? You mentioned drugs."

She just stared at him, wondering how much she'd said. Evidently, too much. "She was a meth addict. Do you know what happens to a baby born to an addict, a meth addict in particular?"

He just shook his head after a moment of considering. "No, can't say I do."

"Well, it's not pretty. The baby is born addicted and spends her first few months being weaned off the drug. Not an ideal baby, a screamer, not one any foster parent wants. Nonetheless, there she is, a nightmare baby, in and out of the ER, passed around from home to home, because a baby like that is difficult to care for and is definitely not wanted. But she cleans up pretty good, doesn't she?"

Why was she talking to him, sharing anything with him? He was not her friend, and this could be something he would use against her down the road. His sympathy was not something she wanted. She pulled her arms across her chest and took in her water when he said nothing, making the situation awkward.

"I don't know what to say," he replied. "Are you sure it's her? I mean, she's an elementary school teacher, with two girls, married to Jim Jackson. Although I don't know her personally, or them, they are friends of the chief and have lived here a long time. The girls were born here, from the checking I did. So, again, are you sure it's her?"

Why was he asking this? She'd basically tipped her hand already, admitting she hadn't really known.

"You heard her," she replied. "I wasn't entirely sure it was her when I knocked on the door this morning, but then, she wasn't easy to find. The last known location I was able to find was here. It's as if she didn't want to be found, and someone went to a great deal of trouble to make sure she wasn't. It's her. I'm entitled to answers."

He said nothing, just looked across the table at her. She wondered what he was going to say. Then she heard the ding of the door, and her stomach knotted as she spotted Carly, wearing heels and makeup and a dark dress as if ready for a party. Then Carly spotted her.

"She's here," was all she got out, hearing the heels click. Mark turned his chair with a scrape and stood.

Carly nodded to him, her lips tight, as he gestured to the chair he'd just been sitting in. "No," she said. "Sorry, but I can't stay. I wanted to stop by and let you know I can't do this."

Billy Jo couldn't make herself get up. She could smell Carly's lavender perfume and see how slender she was from the cut of the dress, expensive, classy. Her earrings were sapphire with diamonds. She held her car keys in her hand. Carly was about to walk away, and she could feel another slap coming.

"No, wait, I don't deserve this," Billy Jo said. "I deserve the truth, answers. Don't walk away from me."

It came out quite sharply, and Carly looked over her shoulder, alarmed. Mark said nothing, just stood there. She wondered when he'd try to shut this down.

"Keep your voice down," Carly said. "You think I want anyone knowing? I have a good life now. I'm sorry for what happened to you, but that's not me, not anymore. I'm leaving here, and I'll ask you just one more time to leave me alone. I'm meeting my husband at a charity event. I'll make your excuses for dinner tomorrow, but let me be clear: I do not want to see you ever again." Her voice was low, her meaning clear. She glanced only once to Mark and said, "Detective."

As she walked away, Billy Jo went to slide back her chair, to stand and go after her, to yell—but Mark suddenly took a step around the table and settled his hand on her shoulder, then leveled her with that look he had.

"No, Billy Jo. Let her go. You want answers, I get it, but this isn't the way," he said. Maybe he realized she wasn't about to go quietly into the night. Then he looked around and let his gaze settle back on her. "You got anything nice to wear?"

She could feel her brows pull together. "Excuse me? What's wrong with what I'm wearing?"

There it was, that smile of his. She knew she was about to walk into something as he said, "Well, there's a charity event at the golf course tonight. It calls for a dress, heels."

"You mean the same event Jim and Carly are going to right now."

Mark said nothing for a second, then, "That would be the one. Say I pick you up in an hour?"

He was serious. She hadn't expected this from him. She reached for her bag and lifted it, then replied, "Forty-five minutes. And, Detective…"

He inclined his head but didn't say anything.

"Thank you," she said.

Chapter 6

Mark had never expected in a million years that Billy Jo could clean up so well. She sat in the passenger side of his Jeep, wearing a soft blue spaghetti-strap dress that stopped just above the knees. She had always hidden her figure in boxy casual clothes, but she couldn't hide it in that dress. She never wore makeup, either. He had to take a second look. She was cute—no, pretty, and wouldn't get lost in a crowd.

Now he had noticed her. Maybe that was why he was pulling at his tie, feeling how tight it was, as he stepped out into the parking lot, wearing a dark suit that he'd never worn once since being on the island. He waited for Billy Jo to walk around in her strappy heels, which added a few inches to her short height. He made himself look away as she tucked something into a small flashy clutch purse, the chain of which she lifted over her shoulder. Her arms were bare.

"There's a lot of really nice vehicles here," she said as they strode to the main clubhouse, seeing the Mercedes parked beside them.

"There's a lot of money on the island." Mark glanced down to Billy Jo as they walked, trying to reconcile her current image with the idea of her as an unwanted baby. Carly Jackson was well off, it seemed, and he just couldn't see her as a meth addict who'd abandoned a baby. "You look really nice, by the way, in case I didn't say it."

Maybe that was a smile she did her best to hide. Then she nudged his arm with hers. "So do you, Detective. Didn't think you owned a suit—but I see you kept your cowboy boots on."

"What's wrong with cowboy boots?"

She tossed him a look. "Well, generally, when you dress up for events like this, you put on a pair of dress shoes."

The way she said it reminded him so much of the way his mom went at his dad at times, but Jed Friessen was as cowboy as they came, and he'd likely be buried with his cowboy boots on. Maybe that was who Mark got it from.

"Yeah, well, don't go sticking me into some mold. Besides, you're the only reason I'm putting myself through this stuck-up fundraiser. And just hold up a second before we go in. Let's be clear on a few things. I get that you're pissed, and I'm not sure how I'd feel, if I were you, about the way she blew you off. This is about showing up, being seen, and letting Carly Jackson know you're not about to go away quietly. It's just about getting answers and an apology, right?"

Billy Jo only shook her head. "Don't worry. I won't embarrass you, and wasn't this your idea, anyway? Pretty sure my just being here and letting Carly see I'm not going to go away will make her realize I don't take no for an answer. I won't be warned away or blown off. We'll go over, say hi, schmooze, and let her freak out a bit. I know it's her, but I guarantee that no one knows what she did, not her husband or anyone in this brand-new life she has."

He didn't know why, but he had the feeling this was about so much more. They walked up the clean carpeted stairs, passing a poster with a picture of an old guy—Van Davidson, a judge or something like that. For a moment, he wondered what Billy Jo's angle would be.

She made a face as she gestured to the poster. "Do you know anything about this charity, this Davidson fundraiser? I mean, what exactly is this party raising money for?"

He found himself really looking at the poster and then the front door, where even the staff were decked out in formal wear. "Not sure." he said. "Seems to be what rich people do here. Start a foundation, a charity, and get together to raise money for something. I didn't ask. You really want to know?"

She dragged her gaze over to him. "As a detective, shouldn't you know what this is really about in case we're asked? I mean, all I had time for was a quick Google of Van Davidson, but apparently, he founded this golf club. He was a senior Second Circuit judge nominated by the first Bush administration. Went to Stanford Law, and prior to his nomination, he was state's attorney. He died five years ago. He had some clout, and it appears he divided his time between his home in Sacramento, where his duties were, and Roche Harbor, where he has a home and where his wife lives."

He didn't know what to say. "And you just Googled all that?"

She shrugged. "My dad is a lawyer, a good one. Worked as what you'd call a fixer in Washington. All the politicians knew him, used him, so I already had an idea. I know how nominations work, senate committees. A judge like that carries weight. The foundation, though, sounds interesting."

He wasn't sure what to make of her remark, picking up

on the sarcasm. A young man dressed in black pants, a red vest, and a white shirt pulled the door open for them.

"Thank you," Billy Jo said as she went in first, whereas Mark was struck by the open room, the high ceiling, and the glass windows that covered every wall. Then there were the voices of the crowd of people, women in dresses and heels, men in suits and tuxes. Formal attire was a given for this kind of shindig.

Mark reached for her arm as he looked around, seeing the kinds of people he never mingled with. "Just hold up a second, Billy Jo. We're here, so how about we set some ground rules? Let's get a drink and say hi. I had no idea you rubbed shoulders with these kinds of people…"

"If the next words out of your mouth are that these are 'my kind' of people, I can assure you they're not. Because of who my dad is, I understand how they think and who they are, and I also understand the fundamentals of law and how this world works. My dad insisted I take pre-law, after all. But although I understand this game, this isn't my life. I wasn't groomed into this. Don't worry, Detective. Let's grab a drink and mingle."

The way she said "mingle," he had the sinking feeling that he was playing a game of cat and mouse, and no one had thought to explain the rules to him. He followed Billy Jo over to the bar, where she ordered a glass of red, and the bartender looked over to him and said, "What can I get you, sir?"

He gestured and said, "Pale ale."

The bartender poured the red wine for Billy Jo and took the cap off his beer.

"No glass," Mark said, waving it off. He pulled his wallet out and tossed down a twenty.

Billy Jo lifted her wine and took a sip as the bartender put his change on the bar. He tossed a coin in the tip glass and shoved the bills in his pocket before reaching for his beer, lifting the bottle to his lips, and taking a long swallow.

"You know, if you're trying to fit in, the beer goes in a glass," Billy Jo said.

He wondered whether she understood what she was saying. "You think I'm the kind of guy who tries to fit in?"

She didn't pull her gaze from him. There was something about this complex woman. She was like an onion, and he was peeling back a layer at a time to see something new underneath.

"No, I guess you're not, though I'm not sure that's in your favor." She nodded behind him. "Your chief has just spotted you. He's standing over there with the Jacksons, Jim and Carly. Guess they really are friends."

He dragged his gaze across the room, seeing the chief and Gail, both decked out. The chief was frowning at him. He held out his arm to Billy Jo and said, "Well, shall we?"

She slid her hand on his arm, and they walked over. Gail was the only one with a warm smile for him and Billy Jo. Either Carly was a great actress or she'd had plenty of practice pretending something didn't bother her.

"Detective and Billy Jo, is it?" Jim said, holding out his hand to Mark and then glancing down at Billy Jo "Didn't know you were attending this fundraiser. Did you know Van?"

Yeah, the man didn't have a clue. Carly still hadn't said anything.

"No," Mark said. "I haven't been here on the island that long. So what exactly is the money going toward?"

The cop in him needed answers.

"It goes to the conservancy," Jim said, "to protect the wetland here. Van donated a part of his land when he died."

"Birds and trees," Mark said. It just rolled off his tongue.

Billy Jo hadn't pulled her gaze from Carly. This could go one of two ways, he thought.

"So it seems my wife knows this young lady's mother," Jim said, looking down at her. "You were friends, right?"

Carly was decked out in a black cocktail dress and heels, and Mark found himself really looking for similarities between her and Billy Jo. She gave a tight smile as she looked up to her husband. There was just something about her. He couldn't understand how she could turn her back on her daughter like that.

"That's right, a long time ago. Seems like another lifetime," she said. "We just haven't had a chance to catch up, is all. Took me by surprise this morning. I didn't remember her at first. I hadn't heard about her in a long time…"

"That's right," Billy Jo said. "We'll talk more tomorrow night, dinner at your house. We can catch up, and you can fill me in about my mother."

Carly smiled, but he could sense the daggers she was throwing at Billy Jo. He had to fight the urge to laugh, because Billy Jo didn't concede to anyone. At least he'd figured out that part of her.

"So how long have you been a teacher?" Billy Jo said.

As they waited for Carly to answer, the chief gestured to Mark and stepped away. He really couldn't sneak anything past him.

"Excuse me," Mark said, then strode off to join the chief.

"So what is going on here?" the chief said. "Jim called me after the incident at the school, saying Ms. McCabe is the daughter of an old friend of his wife. What is it that no one's telling me? You have to know something, because I can tell you, like Jim, I'm wondering what this is really about. And now, with you showing up here for this, I know something's going on."

So Jim wasn't as blind to his wife's situation as he'd first thought. He knew his chief would have a lot of questions about why he was there.

"One thing about living on this island, you said, is that I have to get to know people here," Mark replied. "This seems like a perfect way, so why not come?"

The chief actually chuckled under his breath. "Well, for one, it was invitation only, and the cost for dinner is two hundred dollars per plate. I know what you make, and I can see how uncomfortable you are in that monkey suit. Didn't know you and Ms. McCabe were dating, friends, or whatever this is. Just to be clear, Jim's a friend of mine. We've known him and Carly for a long time. Gail and I are godparents to their girls, Patty and Lisa. With you showing up here with Ms. McCabe, I have to wonder a lot of things. It's not an investigation about a complaint, so what exactly is Ms. McCabe up to? I don't believe she's the daughter of an old friend."

Though Mark was still stuck on the cost of dinner, something about his boss asking this kind of direct question let him know he couldn't blow him off. "Hey, all I can say is Jim overreacted a bit. You heard his wife. She knew Billy Jo's mother. Don't forget that Billy Jo is new to the island, too. She needs to get to know some people."

The chief didn't pull his shrewd gaze. So many things about his boss were a mystery, and he wondered what Tolly Shepard really had his hands in. If he knew one thing about cops, it was that there was always something else going on behind the wall. The line of the law was so subjective.

He made himself look away, knowing his chief was a man he would never want to go up against.

"You just make sure that's all it is," the chief replied. "As I said, Jim is a friend. As for meeting these people, this is the wrong crowd for a social worker. These are not her people, because they won't have any kind of spotlight shone on their families. You understand what I'm saying? If you don't keep Ms. McCabe in line and see that she understands her role on the island and which toes she's not to step on, I will handle her. We clear here?"

He knew it wasn't really a question. He lifted his gaze over to where Billy Jo was standing in an intimate circle with Jim, Carly, and Gail. "Understood," was all he said.

The chief smiled and slapped his arm. "Good, so finish up your beer and make your excuses." He went to step away but stopped. "Oh, and, Mark, next time, I expect a heads up. Don't pull this on me again."

The chief's gaze lingered, and Mark could see the line he'd crossed with his boss.

"As I said," he replied, "this is just a friendly catch-up, a personal thing. She's meeting some locals. I didn't think I needed to clear that with you."

There was no smile from the chief. Mark knew well that this kind of challenge to authority had landed him in hot water time and again. In fact, it was why his career as a cop had ended up with him here.

"Again, my island, my rules," the chief said. "You like your job?"

Mark pulled in a breath and shrugged. "As I said, I understand. We'll finish our drinks and be on our way."

The chief walked off, and Mark took a second, as he lifted his beer to take a drink, to really see these people, their smiles, their monkey suits, the glitz and the money and the secrets.

Secrets and lies in a small town… Maybe he needed to take a closer look at everyone here so he understood clearly whose toes he was stepping on.

Chapter 7

"I don't understand why we had to leave," Billy Jo said.

Something had been off with the detective since his short one-on-one with the chief. She knew well when someone was getting slapped down, and the chief hadn't exactly seemed happy about their arrival.

"You heard the chief when he said we wouldn't be staying for dinner and the auction," Mark said. "I guess I just didn't expect you to go along with it so easily. Besides, wasn't the idea just to show up and let Carly know you're not going away? Pretty sure you accomplished that, so pushing it would've been overkill."

She could feel everything, riding in his Jeep. The roads were far from perfect, but at least he'd thrown out the takeout packaging that was usually at her feet on the floor of the passenger side. She was still surprised at Mark's willingness to show up for her to begin with. There was just something about him that she didn't understand.

"You think I couldn't tell from the chief's expression that he was just waiting to pull you aside and go a round or two with you?" she said. "I get it. At least dinner is on tomorrow, though. You should've seen Carly's face, the way she was staring daggers at me. I swear the woman isn't about to make this easy. Then there's her husband. She's lying to him."

Mark pulled into her place, which was now dark, as the sun had just set. His headlights flashed on her small car and the stairs that led up to her loft. Another Friday night, which she usually spent with Netflix, brownies, wine, and her cat, Harley. The outside light was on.

Mark turned off the Jeep and just sat there for a minute. He seemed to be considering something as he stared out the window, his hand resting on the steering wheel. She unfastened her seatbelt and reached for the handle of the door.

"You think it's a good idea, going for dinner?" he said, looking across the Jeep to her. "I mean, really, what are you trying to get out of this? I get that you're angry. I'm even a little pissed for you. But you said you want answers, so what answers are you looking for? An apology? Because that woman is too terrified and determined to protect the life she has. For one, I can see her husband has no idea. She's not about to apologize. When someone has a secret like that, she'll go to all kinds of lengths to protect it."

What was she supposed to say? For years, she'd thought of her mother, hated her, wanted her, ached for that loss. Now, seeing her and the good life she had made her angrier than she could admit to herself.

Billy Jo gave the handle a yank and stepped out, feeling unsteady in her heels. The chill of the fall air on her bare arms had her pulling in a breath. She wasn't sure what made her look, but as she took in her place and saw a light inside, she couldn't remember leaving it on.

"What's wrong?" Mark asked.

She shook her head. "Inside light is on. I didn't leave it

on. Maybe my landlords were inside…" she said. Then she heard Mark open his door. "What are you doing?"

He was already walking around to her steps. She could see that he'd pulled his tie free and undone his top dress shirt buttons. "Your landlords always go in your place without asking?"

She gave the passenger door a shove closed, clutching the purse she'd used only once, a gift from Rose, her mom, who couldn't help oozing class. "No, but they live just over there, so…" She found herself looking over to their big, beautiful house, seeing a light on over there, as well. The friendliness of Lesley and Lorne was something she was still getting used to.

Mark was already up on the deck. "Well, then I'll just check it out, make sure there isn't a problem, and be on my way," he said. His hand was on the doorknob.

As he opened it, she held the rail and started up behind him, unsure how to deal with a male who thought she needed protecting—her, Billy Jo.

"The door's unlocked," he said, then pulled a gun she hadn't known had been tucked in his waistband, at his back. He was already inside her house as she stepped up on the deck and took in her cat, who was hopping to the door. The light spilled out.

"I always leave my door unlocked," she called out to him. "That's not the issue here."

As she stepped inside, Mark was walking back into her kitchen, tucking his gun back in his waistband. Evidently, he'd just been in her bedroom. She slipped off her heels and gave her purse a toss onto the small sofa, which added a western flair to the suite. Harley was hopping her way, and she leaned down and picked him up, feeling him purr against her.

"Well, doesn't look as if anyone's been here," he said,

walking around the island, looking at everything. What was it about this man? He was an absolute mystery. "You seriously leave your door unlocked? Not smart, you know. Anyone could just walk in."

"As I said, it must've been my landlords," she said. "Really, this isn't the big city. It's an island. What am I worried about? Lesley and Lorne live right there, and they know when I'm home and when I'm not. I can't tell you the number of times I've woken up to Lesley coming over in the morning with freshly baked muffins. They can see anyone coming, so who's really going to drive out here and break in?"

He looked around her place again before letting his gaze settle on the bottle of red wine on the island, then on Harley. "Why a three-legged cat?" he said.

"You want a glass of wine?"

He only shrugged. "Is that the only way you'll answer?"

She wondered whether he was teasing her. She set Harley down at his food bowl and walked around to the cupboard, which she pulled open. She reached for a wine glass and held it up. "No, that's my way of saying I'm having a glass of wine, so do you want one?"

She didn't think he could smile, but there it was, the pull at his lips. "Fine, why not?" He gestured toward the bottle, and she twisted off the cap and filled two glasses. "So what happened to your cat, an accident or something?" He reached for one of the glasses and lifted it, then swirled it before taking a swallow.

She wasn't sure what to make of his expression. She flicked her gaze to her own wine and took a sip, watching Harley hop across the room to the hewn wood sofa she knew Lorne Lancaster had made.

"When I got him, I heard he'd been hit by a car and

dumped at the shelter," she said. "I worked part-time there in school. They took his leg off and saved him, but that was only after I insisted. Otherwise, they were planning to just euthanize him. He was unwanted, unclaimed. I knew the feeling too well. One of the shelter workers said he wasn't worth it, because who was going to cover the cost of the vet bill? So I did. I paid it, I took him, and I've had him ever since."

The way he was watching her was making her uncomfortable. She took another swallow and gave him her back as she walked over to the sofa, where Harley had managed to jump up and was tucking himself in to sleep at one end. She sat next to him and rested her hand on him.

"Makes sense," Mark said.

She wasn't sure what to make of that. "What does?"

He was leaning on the island. He downed the rest of the wine and let out a sigh before setting his empty glass down. There was just something about Mark: She never knew where he was coming from. "Why you are the way you are," he said. "I know when someone is fighting something—demons, baggage, anger. There's something there. It's why you got in the business you did, helping kids. Not that I'm saying there's anything wrong with that. It's noble. But the way you come at everyone… I swear you'd walk right into a storm anyone else would take shelter from. You make nothing easy. You're like a puzzle with a lot of missing pieces."

She didn't lift her hand from her cat. She could feel the fight starting to stir inside her.

"Now, don't get all pissed," he said. "Everyone has something. But this whole thing with Carly Jackson, what are you trying to get out of it? To destroy her, take a chunk out of her, get some payback? If that's it, I get it. I understand. Just make sure you know what you want, because from where I'm standing, the answers you find may not be the ones you're looking for. Once you know something, you know it. No going back."

His blue eyes were filled with seriousness. Did he have any idea how much she had wondered the same about him, why he did what he did, why he was the way he was?

"You know," she said, "when I was four, someone told me the best thing that could've happened to me was to die as a baby. They say when you're that young, you don't remember things, but I remember everything. The house where I was living was a yellow rancher, and I shared a room with two other foster girls. My foster mother was overweight, always wearing a housecoat. Her husband watched me in a way I'll never forget. He never said much. It was just this look, this awful feeling that he hated me. It was then I felt the fear a child should never feel. I mean, who says that to a little kid? So yeah, maybe I do go around saving things, animals and kids that others toss away, because I know what it's like to feel unwanted, a nuisance, someone of no importance. It never goes away, that memory. So if you're worried about me hearing something bad from Carly, I guarantee you nothing she could say would make my memories worse."

He lowered his gaze and twisted the cap off the wine, then walked over to her. He waited in front of her as she held out her glass, which still had a splash in it. He filled it halfway and then rested the bottle on the sofa table.

"So tomorrow night, dinner at Carly and Jim's," he said. "You know they have kids?"

She didn't nod as she stared up at him, wondering what this was. She flicked her gaze back down to her wine. "Of course I know they have kids, two girls."

He nodded and started walking to the door before stopping and turning back to her. "What time is dinner?"

She slid around on the sofa. Something about the way he was looking at her should have bothered her. "Why?" she said, feeling the familiar distrust.

He shook his head. "You think I'm letting you walk in there yourself? For one, the chief would have my head on a platter. I know you wouldn't hurt those girls, but your anger toward Carly might."

She forced herself to swallow back her outrage, her first response of no. "I wouldn't do that, not in front of them."

He only nodded. "Well, then you'll have no problem with me there. Pick you up at five tomorrow."

She pulled her tongue over her front teeth. "Jerk," she said under her breath.

"Is that a yes? Can't wait."

There it was, his arrogance.

"Make it quarter to," she said, "and don't look so happy, because although I wouldn't cause a scene in front of the kids, I do plan on making it very clear to Carly that I'll be getting my answers, my pound of flesh, and then…" She didn't have a clue.

Mark only inclined his head as she stopped talking. He took a step toward her, giving her that all-cop gaze she figured he had mastered. "And what, Billy Jo? What do you expect to happen, a happily ever after, an apology? What exactly are you looking for?"

There it was, the million-dollar question.

"Goodnight, Mark," was all she said.

He lingered another second, then pulled open the door and tossed her one last look. For a moment, she thought he was about to add something else, but he only yanked open the door and stepped out.

"Lock the door behind me," he said. Then he was gone.

She rested her full glass of wine on the sofa table and listened to his footsteps on the stairs, the door of his Jeep, the engine starting. She took in the now closed door and got up to flick the lock.

What was it about Mark Friessen? At times, his personality had her wanting to scratch his eyes out, yet here he was, helping her. Or was he babysitting her?

Whatever it was, she didn't want to think too long and hard on it, because tomorrow she planned to make the woman who had created her childhood nightmare feel just a tad of what she'd endured. She'd expected to feel some sort of closure, pleasure, happiness—but instead, all she could feel was the ache of being unwanted, which had existed in her heart forever. The wound she thought had healed cracked open again.

Chapter 8

Mark heard the car before he saw it, leaning in the open doorway of his cabin, holding a steaming black coffee. That mangy mutt of a dog was wandering through the overgrown weeds outside, lifting his leg, as the sun crept up over the horizon.

He took in the black pickup with the sheriff's logo, which pulled up and parked. The dog gave a bark and ran over to the chief just as he stepped out, wearing a ballcap, sunglasses, and a gray jacket labeled "Police."

"Hey there, doggy." The chief ran his hand over the dog's head, down to its wagging tail, then started toward where Mark stood.

"Here kind of early, Chief," he said. The chief showing up at his cabin at the crack of dawn let him know something was up.

"Figured you and I need to have a talk."

He could have asked about what, and he was tempted to, but he already knew. "You want coffee?" He held up his mug.

The chief only shook his head. "Nope, Gail's got me

off coffee and on green tea. Can you imagine such a thing? I swear her and the doctor are trying to kill me."

He would've smiled, but there was something about the man he took orders from that put him on edge. He found himself always wondering how things would be handled.

"This isn't a social call, Mark," the chief said.

"Didn't think it was."

There it was, the odd smile. Chief Shepard didn't pull his gaze or take off his sunglasses as he stopped at the open deck, resting his foot on it. He really was a big man, and Mark had never felt more like a visitor to the island than he did then. "Then let's get right to it. What's that little lady up to?"

He lifted his mug and took another swallow as the dog wandered over to him and then inside the open door. He could hear him lapping up water from his bowl. He didn't miss the way the chief tracked him. "I think you're going to need to be a little more specific. I presume we're talking about Billy Jo McCabe, the social worker."

The chief pulled his sunglasses off, and the iciness in his eyes reminded Mark of a chilly day. Chief Tolly Shepard was a man one didn't mess with. "Stop playing games, Mark. You know damn well I'm talking about Billy Jo, and I also know you know what she's up to, what she's doing, what she wants with the Jacksons. You and I both know that story last night about her being the daughter of a friend of Carly's is total, complete horse-shit. You think I didn't know everything about Ms. McCabe before she was assigned here—the who, what, why, and where? You think I don't know who's being sent here? I signed off on her, just like I did you, though I can tell by your face that you don't believe me. Just like you, Mark, I know her deep, dark secrets. You think I want some wildcard showing up here and thinking she has the right to go all cowboy, believing she can change how things are run?"

The chief glanced back to the dog, who trotted out and lay on the wooden deck. Mark sensed that the chief maybe knew more about him than he was comfortable with.

"You have a way about you, Mark," the chief said. "You don't say a word, and those who don't know you think you'll just go along with things, except you don't." He pointed toward him. "I'm waiting."

Mark finished the last of his coffee. "Some of it isn't my story to tell."

"You mean like how Ms. McCabe was a ward of the state of Nevada until she was fifteen, when she was adopted by Chase and Rose McCabe, with numerous criminal charges for weapons, solicitation, robbery, and assault? Now she shows up on this island, on Jim and Carly's doorstep. Jim doesn't buy the story about his wife suddenly remembering a long-lost friend's daughter, so what is this really about? Your showing up with Ms. McCabe last night at the golf course, even I could see how that was meant to needle at Carly Jackson—and it worked. It got under her skin. She was off all night. So I'll ask one more time: What is this really about?"

So Jim Jackson didn't believe his wife.

"Just like Billy Jo said, it's about her mother," Mark replied. "She's just looking for answers, is all."

"And Carly Jackson has them, is that what you're saying?"

He could feel that the chief was putting all his pieces in place, and he wondered why he was so interested in the personal details of this. Maybe there was more to the relationship between Jim and his chief than he knew.

"She does," Mark said. "At the same time, Chief, this isn't a police matter…"

"Oh, that's where you're wrong, Mark. When it comes to my island and the people here, if someone is looking to rattle their cages and stir things up, I'll make sure it's shut down. What goes on in this community is very much police business. Now, Jim has made himself clear that he doesn't want trouble on his doorstep, and Ms. McCabe, like you, tends to stir things up rather than following along with how things have been done since the beginning of time. So what's the real story between Ms. McCabe and Jim's wife?"

He knew he squinted. Dinner tonight was now feeling much like a game of cat and mouse. He was walking a fine line and could end up hurting a family. "It's about Billy Jo's mother," he said, "her real mother. She just wants answers."

It seemed everything he told the chief would go right back to Jim Jackson, but there was an opportunity here for him to get some info behind the scenes on the relationship between Jim and Carly.

"How long have the Jacksons been married, lived here?" he said.

The chief could be a hard man to read. "Jim's family has been on the island for two generations, off and on. They go off to school and then come back. He's been married to Carly over ten years, a long time. But I'm starting to think there's something going on with Carly, and her husband is too. He's a smart man. Ms. McCabe's arrival has upset his wife. I understand you're going for dinner at the Jacksons' tonight."

He just had this feeling that there was more to come. There always was with the chief. Maybe that was why he was really there on his doorstep.

"We are," he said, then looked in his empty mug, feeling the need for a second cup.

"Good. When you're there, I want you to find out what Carly Jackson is up to, what she's hiding. Then there's Ms. McCabe. The way she's pushed this thing with Carly tells me it isn't a simple trip down memory lane. She's up to something. She wants something, and I want to know what."

He'd never figured the chief would expect him to spy and report back. How little did he know him? "Chief, I can assure you this is just a personal matter for Billy Jo. She's just looking for answers about her mother. She has some questions and is hoping Carly can answer them, is all." He knew that wasn't what the chief had asked of him. He was playing with fire with a man who could end his career permanently.

"You think you're smarter than me, Mark, but you're not. You wonder why you were turned down from seven county sheriff's stations until taking a job out here was your only option? No one wanted you. You were a disgrace to the blue wall. Next time, you'll be looking for a new line of work, or you'll find yourself in a pine box. Telling your parents they've lost a son isn't something I want. I'll fire you first."

He reminded himself to give nothing as he pulled in a breath. "The island wasn't my only option."

"No, but being stationed to Alaska with no backup, facing down some of the worst, most violent criminals, doesn't sound like much of a choice. The only reason you're here, working here, is because of me. Whistle-blowers lose everything, Mark. I gave you a second chance, and this is it. Don't you let me down, boy, because this isn't a game. When I ask you to do something, you do it."

There it was, the reminder, all because he'd done the right thing once.

"As I said, Chief, all I know is that Billy Jo is looking for answers on her mother. If Carly's hiding something, I have no idea what it is. It's sounding to me as if Jim Jackson doesn't trust his wife, and maybe he shouldn't, but again, what do I know? I'm just doing what you said, keeping the peace and making sure Billy Jo doesn't go off the reservation, as you put it. I'm reining her in, making sure toes aren't stepped on. Tonight, we'll go for dinner. Carly and Billy Jo will talk, catch up, and that'll be the end of it." He didn't like feeling as if he were expected to be exactly who the chief told him to be.

"You just make sure it is, Mark. This is your second chance."

He let his hand fall to his side, still holding his empty mug, "You seem to forget that I refuse to look the other way just because it's expected of me, Chief," Mark said. "You know that about me. You said you admired it."

The man actually smiled at him, then gave his head a shake. "You have integrity, Mark, which can be a good thing until it's not." He gestured to the dog, who was still lying on the deck with his head down. "You give that dog a name yet?"

So that was it. His message had been delivered, apparently.

"Told you he's not my dog. Can't name him."

The chief simply stepped away from the deck and started back to his pickup. He gave the door a yank and pulled it open, then hesitated after slipping his sunglasses back on. "I'm doing eighteen holes this morning. I need you to man the phones in the office. Gail's off island at a doctor's appointment."

Then the chief climbed in his truck and started it. Mark considered the warning, remembering all the toes he'd stepped on to get himself here. The first thing he'd been taught as a wet-behind-the-ears cop was to never,

ever go against a fellow officer, no matter what he believed the truth was. *Whatever an officer puts in a report is the truth, no matter what, so help you God.*

Yet here he was now, on an island he'd never expected to be on, all because he hadn't looked the other way.

Chapter 9

"Pam, I'm leaving to go for dinner," Billy Jo called out to the small and mostly empty office as she slid her files and notes into her bag. Tonight, she'd finish typing up her latest report on a complaint about a kid. It was from a neighbor, apparently, and the allegations were alarming.

"Hey, Grant is holding on the line for you," Pam replied, peeking around the corner into Billy Jo's cubby. Her dark hair was pulled back, and she wore freshly applied pink lipstick and a casual light brown sweater. "He says he tried your cell phone, but it went to voicemail."

Billy Jo reached in her bag and pulled her cell phone out, seeing that the battery was dead. "Suppose you can't tell him you missed me and I'm now gone for the day?"

Pam's dimples popped. "Grant would have my head on a platter. Besides, I already told him you were still here. Just take the call." She strode away in her purple yoga pants, curvy, a mother of three, twenty years her senior. Pam had run the office for over ten years.

Billy Jo reached for the phone at her desk, seeing the

line blinking, and pressed the button. "Hi, Grant. What can I do for you?" She pulled her charger from her bag and plugged her phone in.

"Well, for one, maybe you can explain why it's just been brought to my attention that a sealed file on Billy Jo Thornton has been accessed using your password and login details. You mind telling me why you're accessing that personal file?"

Was he kidding? How would he have found out, though? They all, including Grant, accessed all kinds of files just because they could.

"Billy Jo Thornton was me, Grant," she said. "What's the big deal, really? I have a right to the information in there. That's my information."

"Yeah, actually, you don't. The information is owned by the state of Nevada—you know, a government agency, like the kind you work for? Do you have any idea the number of laws you've broken, accessing something for personal use?" Was he really having this conversation with her?

"Grant, you and I both know that accessing closed files is something everyone does. Even you've done it. How did you even know about me opening that file to begin with? I had questions." She wondered if Pam was listening. She could hear her on the other side of the cubby, though she should've been long gone by now.

"Well, lucky for you, I heard from my boss, who heard from his boss—which is beside the point, because evidently, you were flagged. Why are you looking at it? What's going on?"

She shut her eyes and pressed her fingers to the bridge of her nose, pulling in another breath. "I was just curious, is all. I had a question, so I opened it, read it. I really didn't think it was a big deal." She wondered why the lie rolled off her tongue so easily.

There was silence on the other end.

"Fine," he finally said. "I get it, but stop. Seems someone is watching, so take a word of advice: No more looking for anything you shouldn't. I've also been advised to issue a letter of warning to you. I'm not sure whose chain you jerked, but consider yourself reprimanded."

She just shook her head, thinking of the file she'd accessed. She'd taken screenshots, which she'd saved to her laptop. Maybe she should take another look, but the thought of having to read all the notes again, the lies and accusations… Even the one foster parent she'd actually liked had said bad things about her, and the realization had slammed her in the stomach much worse than any fist ever could.

"I won't access it again. Is that everything?" she said, though even she could hear how sharply it had come out. Not smart. "Sorry, Grant. Look, I'm running late and honestly never thought it would be a big deal."

She heard tapping on the other end. Then he pulled in a breath and said, "Duly noted. I don't remember seeing today's report from you, by the way. There was a complaint about a baby. You make it out there?"

The complaint hadn't come from the police department, she recalled, so it had been marked with instructions for her to check it out. But she had a dinner tonight. "I'm going first thing in the morning," she said.

"Tonight would be better."

She glanced at her watch, seeing it was already four. She'd planned on stopping at home and changing.

"The note I have from Pam says the allegations are serious enough that you should stop in tonight," he said. "There's fear for the baby's safety."

"And the police weren't called? Pam called you? Because that's not the information I got." She knew Pam was listening, and she felt sucker punched by someone she should have respected.

"Nope, just a complaint to social services," Grant said. "Go check it out. If warranted, take the baby." It wasn't lost on her that he'd said nothing about Pam.

"Fine, I'll go now," she said.

Grant didn't say anything else before hanging up. She settled the phone in its cradle, then reached for her cell phone and charger and dumped them back in her bag.

"Pam!" she called out. It came out quite sharply, too.

Pam appeared a second later, not smiling anymore. By the way she looked at her, Billy Jo had never realized there could be an issue there.

"Look, I don't appreciate you going to Grant behind my back about the baby," she said. "I remember clearly the allegation you gave to me. You told me to check it out later when I have time."

She seemed to stand her ground. It was there in her expression. "I think you misunderstood, Billy Jo. That wasn't quite what I said. Maybe your focus is not on the job but elsewhere, on personal stuff."

For a second, she had to remind herself how long Pam had been there, running the office. Although Billy Jo wasn't her boss, maybe she needed to keep a closer eye on her.

"Yeah, well, every time a request comes in now, you're going to be filing it in a report to me in writing. No more telling me verbally, because if a baby is at risk and you pull this on me, anything that happens is on you."

She knew her remark hit its mark by the way Pam's face flushed. She expected an apology, but instead she said nothing for a moment, then pulled in a breath.

"The family lives in poverty," Pam said. "The

complainant said the mother was going to drown the baby, her firstborn."

Billy Jo lifted her bag over her shoulder. "You didn't tell me the mother was going to drown the baby! Those are important details. I'm leaving now. If I have to take the baby, do we have a home where it can go tonight? Can you at least do that much?" She was still trying to understand everything that had just happened. She realized Pam could've known about her accessing the file, and maybe everything else. Maybe she was the one who'd been watching.

"I'll make a call and find one," she said.

Billy Jo didn't wait for her to say anything else. "See that you do, and send me a text with the details."

She started out of the office, flicked open the deadbolt, and pulled her keys from her bag. That was just something they did now, locking the office door, because one too many social workers had ended up dead after raging parents entered their offices. She listened to the click and then made her way to her car, knowing she still had to charge her phone, feeling the angst of being rushed. She could still feel the knife in her back. Dinner was important, but more so was a baby.

She pulled out of the small parking lot, heading toward the address, but when she spotted Mark's Jeep in front of the sheriff's office, she pulled in and parked beside it, then climbed out. She entered the station and spotted him at his desk, on the phone. He nodded to her, and she took in the empty office as he hung up.

"You're here early," he said. "Was picking you up in half an hour."

She listened to the chair squeak as he sighed and stood up. "I actually have to make a stop first, a complaint about a baby. I may have to take it."

He was already opening his drawer and pulling out his gun to fasten it to his belt. Keys in hand, he walked her way.

"What are you doing?" she said.

"Sounds like you need some police backup. I'll tag along. We can go to the Jacksons' after—or, better yet, maybe we cancel dinner." He was at the door already and pulled it open, then held it for her. Something about his expression told her there was something on his mind.

"How about we don't give Carly a reason to blow me off?" she said. "You think a second dinner invite will be coming? Because I don't. We'll go check on the baby, and hopefully it isn't the worst-case scenario."

He followed her out. She had started to her door, but he gestured to his Jeep. "And if it is?"

"Then I guess you get your wish, and dinner is canceled. But how about I drive?"

Mark reached for his sunglasses and slid them on. He said nothing for another second, then gave his head a shake and did the one thing she hadn't expected: He walked around to the passenger side of her vehicle and said, "Well, are we going?"

She pulled open her door. "Wow. Didn't expect you'd give in so easily."

He gave the passenger door a yank and rested his hand on the doorframe. "Consider this a one-time thing. I've had all the fights I want to get into today."

Chapter 10

He gestured ahead. "Next right. You said Brenda Burns, is it?" She'd shown him the note and the address she'd scribbled down, and all he'd done was nod.

"Yeah, a complaint from a neighbor, Cecily Tucker, who's convinced Ms. Burns is going to hurt her baby." She pulled down the gravel driveway, seeing a small house and a bigger one in the distance. She jammed her foot on the brake to slow down.

Mark gestured ahead again. "Here, pull up, the first house."

"Is this one property?" She didn't see any house numbers, just the one by the road.

"Yeah. There's often more than one house per address on the island."

She took in how cramped he appeared in the front seat of her Corolla, still wondering about his earlier comment. Who was he fighting with?

She parked beside a small white pickup in the dirt in

front of the small house. Mark was out of the car before she'd turned it off, and she followed him, taking in the house, which appeared neat and tidy, one story, maybe a thousand square feet. Mark was looking around at everything, the property, the house, the land. No one was around.

She strode up to the door, her keys still in hand and her bag in the car. She glanced back once to Mark before knocking, and she could hear him come up behind her as she heard footsteps.

The inside door opened to reveal a young woman with long dark hair, who appeared to be of First Nations descent. She pushed open the screen door and said, "Yes?"

How old was she, and from which tribe? Billy Jo could hear the faint cry of a baby in the background.

"I'm Billy Jo McCabe, with social services. I'm looking for Brenda Burns."

Her expression was pissed, and she shook her head. Billy Jo thought the young woman swore, too. "I'm Brenda. What is this about?" She made no motion to move or invite them in.

"Can we come in, please? A complaint has been filed against you. You have a baby?"

Brenda stepped back and motioned them in, though Billy Jo could feel the anger resonating through her. "Let me guess," she said. "The complaint came from Cecily Tucker, right?"

Billy Jo stepped inside and glanced back only once to Mark, who was looking over her head into the small house. Laundry was being folded on the table, and there were dirty dishes on the counter. The TV was on in the small living room, there were a few coats tossed on the floor, and the room looked like it could use a good sweeping. The small kitchen table was filled with clutter, and the new mom appeared tired.

"So you know Ms. Tucker?" Billy Jo said. "Can I see the baby?" She could hear it fussing.

Brenda was barefoot, wearing black sweats and a loose long-sleeved top. She strode across the room to a bassinet, where the baby was propped up. "Well, this is unbelievable. Yeah, I know Cecily. She's my husband's mother. Let me guess: She said I was going to hurt the baby, right?"

She turned to Mark, who was right behind her.

Brenda looked over to him, as well, to the badge he didn't try to hide. "You brought the police too? This keeps getting better and better." She bent down and lifted the still baby, who was wearing light blue pajamas.

"It's just procedure is all, when a complaint is filed," Billy Jo added, noting that Mark hadn't pulled his gaze from the baby. "So Cecily isn't a neighbor?"

Brenda nodded behind her. "Sure, if you want to call her that. She lives in the big house behind this one, but she's my husband's mother."

"Boy or girl?" Mark cut in, still staring at the baby.

"Tate is my son. He's three weeks tomorrow, and as you can see, he's fine. Well, as fine as can be expected, considering he's paralyzed because of the doctor. Yes, the doctor screwed up in delivery, injured his neck, and now my son pays the price. So is that what this is about? I made noise at the hospital because the doctor screwed up, and now you're here?"

Billy Jo didn't know why, but this bothered her more than anything. She stared at the baby and then looked around again at the small house. "I don't know anything about what happened at the hospital. All I was told is that a complaint came in from your neighbor. That's it. So is Tate your first baby?"

The young woman looked over to her. "Yes, he is."

"And where's your husband? Do you have help?"

There was something in her expression, for a moment, that Billy Jo could relate to. "Maybe we should get right to it," she said. "I'm tired. I have a newborn, but not just any newborn. My baby can't kick his legs, and the paralysis will affect his breathing and eating. He won't talk. My husband and I are coping, but he's at work right now. He's a delivery driver. I can assure you I have no intention of hurting my baby, so could you tell me exactly what complaint was filed and what this is about?"

This wasn't exactly what she'd expected. "Did you tell your mother-in-law that you were going to drown the baby or yourself, maybe? I can see you have your hands full. This would be a lot for anyone to handle."

Brenda had her hand over the baby and was rubbing his stomach. She strode over to the table and picked up a cell phone. "You do realize it was a dream?" she said, staring right at them, dragging her gaze over to Mark and then back to Billy Jo. "Yes, that's right. Cecily had a dream that I walked into the ocean with Tate in my arms and was going to drown us because my son is paralyzed. So which of you wants to hear the message she left?"

Mark reached for the cell phone, maybe because Billy Jo was too shocked to say anything.

"The passcode is four one seven eight," Brenda said. "There's only one saved message there. Put it on speaker. Let's have a listen." She was so matter of fact.

Billy Jo didn't have a clue what to say as she glanced over to Mark and then back to Brenda. "A dream."

Brenda only shrugged.

Mark thumbed in the code, his expression unreadable.

"Brenda, I'm so very upset with you," Cecily said over the speaker. "I woke up this morning after dreaming last night that you were at the end of your rope. You walked into the ocean with the baby and killed him, killed yourself. You have to stop. I can't let you kill him, no matter what. My son was devastated. You destroyed the family. You hurt everyone. The baby, he doesn't deserve to die. I begged Trent not to marry you, and he didn't listen, and here we are…"

Brenda actually reached over and hit the end button. "I really don't think you need to hear anything else. She goes on about what a mistake it was to marry someone like me, and he could have done so much better, and he should take the baby and come back home and send me on my way."

"It was a dream she had?" Billy Jo finally cut in.

Brenda's expression was unsmiling, but she was handling it better than Billy Jo would've. "Yes, a dream. It's what she does. Maybe you'd like to call my husband now so he can tell you about his kook of a mother, who's still angry that her son married someone like me. I'll never forget her face when he introduced me to her the first time. She asked me if my people are all drunks and addicts, collecting welfare. Yes, all those myths and stereotypes some people believe are what Trent's mother embraces as gospel.

"He tends to ignore her phone calls. He told me to delete her message, but now, with both of you landing on my doorstep, I figure it's time we moved. We'll find a new place no matter what it costs. This is her property. She owns all this, and the rent is cheap, but this isn't worth it. So no, I do not intend to drown my baby or myself. Or do you investigate allegations based on someone's dream? Is that what we're doing here?"

Billy Jo realized Brenda was waiting for her to answer. She couldn't believe how calm she was being about it. If it had been her, she'd likely have clawed Cecily's eyes out, then yelled and screamed at everyone. "No, we don't investigate dreams," she finally said. "A dream, really? I am so sorry. Unfortunately, though, because an allegation was made, I still have to do a report. I'll have to talk with Cecily, as well." It would become a mark in the file against Brenda even though the complaint was unfounded.

She expected Brenda to scream and yell, to argue, but all she did was shrug. She seemed resigned to it. "Be my guest. Oh, and when you speak with her, ask her to stop looking in the windows. She's always sneaking down here and peeking in."

Billy Jo only nodded.

Mark touched her arm. "We should go," he said to her, then looked over to Brenda. "Sorry to bother you, ma'am, and sorry about your baby." He handed her cell phone back to her and let his gaze linger on Tate. Then he pulled a card from his pocket and rested it on the table. "If your mother-in-law becomes a nuisance or more of a problem, here's my card."

Billy Jo set her card on the table, too. "If you need anything," she said, "give me a call, even just to talk, because there are services available and help for your son. That's what I'm here for."

Brenda offered a tight smile, and Billy Jo only glanced at the cluttered table and took one last look at the house, planning to kick Pam and whoever else hadn't asked more questions, before she followed Mark out the door and down the steps.

They stopped at her car. "You know what?" she said. "We still have time. Let's go over to the other house and have a word with Cecily so I can close this file."

Mark rested his hand on the roof of the car, taking in the house they'd just walked out of, and said, "You hang back a second. Let me go have a word with Cecily and explain to her what happens when reports are made based on something other than fact."

Then he started walking away, over to the big house. Something about Mark seemed off today, not the same arrogant cop she was used to.

Chapter 11

"Are you planning on telling me what you said to Cecily?" Billy Jo said. "Because I have to add it to the report I'll be typing up tonight."

Something about riding in the passenger side of a small compact with someone else behind the wheel put him on edge. Mark didn't trust anyone's driving until he got to know that person. Also, he was still bothered by the way Brenda had looked at him and the situation she'd found herself in.

"Yeah, according to Cecily, her dreams are prophecies." He took in the street Billy Jo was driving up. The clock in her car said they were ten minutes late.

"Prophecies… You're kidding, right?"

He only shook his head, remembering the older woman, her light hair, her blue eyes, and the small yappy dog she had held the entire time he was there in her nice house, with its open floor plan and photos everywhere of family.

"Nope," he said. "She's convinced Brenda is going to hurt the baby. 'She won't be able to cope with a damaged baby'—those were her exact words. Seems the doctor messed up in delivery, a difficult one, according to Cecily, and now the baby has a bleak future that she believes the woman her son married isn't up to. I issued her a warning that dreams are not a reason to call and file a complaint. I'm sure you'll have to go back and visit again, though." He glanced over at Billy Jo as she geared down and slowed, pulling up in front of a nice two-story home with a BMW in the driveway.

She stopped and pulled up the emergency brake. "Unfortunately, that's how it works. A complaint was filed, so there'll always be a black mark against Brenda even though it was unfounded. At least I can go back now and try to offer some solutions. There are programs and some funding available to help the baby. Not much, but it's something, and many don't know about it." She turned off the car.

Mark considered for a moment that Cecily would likely always pose a problem for that young woman. "When you go back, you may want to have a word with the couple. As Brenda said, they need to find another place to live, away from Cecily. Although I can issue her all kinds of warnings, it's still her property. If that couple wants peace, they need to move far away. As far as her looking in the windows, although completely creepy, I can't do anything about it. Again, it's her property."

He climbed out of the small car and took in Billy Jo, who was now walking around the front, then the Jacksons' house. Just another problem. That seemed to be what had defined his entire day.

"I can suggest it, but the reality is, Mark, that they have a baby who's going to need all kinds of support. That costs money. Her husband is a delivery driver, so likely making minimum wage. Housing costs a lot and is not readily available. Cecily is his mother, so it seems to me that if he won't stand up to her and put an end to this nonsense, who is he going to stand up to? That baby of theirs is going to need an advocate, and if the husband just dismisses this, then I guess that says everything about him."

He picked up on the jab, realizing they could go on all night about that call. "You ready for this?" he said instead, tilting his head toward the house as he followed her up the driveway, taking in the carefully manicured lawn, the gardens.

"I've been waiting for this my whole life."

He reached for her arm. "Just hold up. Remember, Billy Jo, they have kids in there."

Her expression reminded him she didn't like being told what to do. "I would never hurt someone's kids, even hers," she said quite directly.

The door opened before she could say anything else.

"Weren't sure you were still coming," said Carly Jackson, her dark hair brushed straight, wearing blue and white slacks and a light blouse, unsmiling, tense. Exactly the kind of greeting he was familiar with as a cop.

"Sorry, just had a bit of a work emergency, but we're here now. You remember the detective."

"Mark Friessen," he said, holding his hand out. Whatever Billy Jo was feeling, he sensed neither really knew a lot about the other. As Carly shook his hand, he could hear voices inside.

"Um, before you come in…" Carly said. "Please. My family doesn't know, and I'd like to keep it that way. I don't want an awkward situation. We'll have dinner, and then you'll leave."

She stepped out of the house and kept her voice low. At least now there was no denying who she was, but he didn't miss the hint of fear. He glanced once to Billy Jo and could see how pissed off she was. She wasn't out to destroy a family—at least, he hoped not.

"Just a friendly dinner, right?" he said. "Then maybe you and Billy Jo can make some time to talk alone."

Carly hesitated and made a motion he thought indicated her agreement. Then she stepped back. "Come in. We're having meatloaf tonight."

So that was it. He followed Billy Jo inside the warm entrance, taking in the light wood, the stairs going up to a second level, and the living room off to the right. He realized his cowboy boots would have to come off, not something he normally did. He reached down and pulled off one, then the other.

"Hey, I see you both made it," said Jim with a bold smile from behind the island, where he was tossing a salad. "Welcome, Mark, Billy Jo."

There was a long wooden table with a bench on one side and chairs on the other. Plates were ready to be set, along with glasses and a bottle of red wine. A bottle of red was open on the counter, as well.

"And these are our girls, Patty and Lisa," Carly said with a smile. The two little girls leaned against her, her hand resting protectively over them.

"Mark, can I get you a beer or wine?" Jim said, pulling open the fridge, while he vaguely heard Billy Jo say something to one of the girls

"Would prefer a beer," he replied.

Jim pulled out two and twisted off the cap of one before handing it to Mark. The kitchen was nice, and he only glanced a second to see the polite discussion between Billy Jo and Carly.

"So how long have you been living on the island, Mark?"

"Coming up on two years, give or take," he said.

Two years since his world had crumbled when he hadn't done the one thing his fellow cops had done: look the other way. But then, he hadn't been raised that way.

"Yeah, I remember when Tolly said he was bringing in a new detective to Roche Harbor from the city," Jim said.

He should clear up the mistake. It hadn't been a city but a county sheriff's office with a staff of fifteen. But what did it matter? "New start, new place, fresh eyes," Mark said.

There it was, a smile and a subtle laugh. "Yeah, definitely needed that after the last guy."

He wasn't sure what to make of the comment, considering no one had said anything to him about the detective he'd replaced. Instead of answering, he lifted his beer and took a swallow.

Jim glanced over to his wife, and if the chief hadn't stopped by that morning and said what he had about Jim not believing Carly, Mark likely would've missed whatever was there in his expression. "So how long have you and Billy Jo McCabe been together?" Jim said.

He'd just taken a swig of his beer, and he choked at the comment. "Went down the wrong way," he sputtered, fisting his hand and pounding his chest a couple times. He didn't miss the amusement in Jim's expression. "Uh, we're actually not together. We're just friends," he finally said.

He couldn't readily think of another word that applied in a situation like this. He found himself looking over, seeing Billy Jo talking with the two girls, helping them set the table. Carly was no longer there.

"Of course you are," Jim said.

His tone had Mark rolling his shoulders and having to bite back the urge to tell him that Billy Jo wasn't his type. Curvy, nasty, and liable to eventually break his heart were more what he gravitated toward.

The oven dinged.

"Dinner's ready, Carly," Jim called out, and Mark stepped away as he pulled open the oven and lifted out the meatloaf.

All Mark could do was take in the smile on Billy Jo's face, realizing that she was with her siblings, only the two girls had no idea.

"Sorry about that," Carly said as she strode back in. She reached for the open bottle of wine on the island and filled one of the four glasses. "Okay, girls, go wash up."

Time for dinner at the Jacksons' and what felt like a game of Clue, where everyone had a secret.

He strode over to Billy Jo, who was staring daggers at Carly, and nudged her with his elbow. She jerked her head up to him. He could see about how well this could go.

When Carly walked over with two glasses of wine and held one out to Billy Jo, he didn't think she'd take it for a second. Then she did, and "Thank you" was all she said.

"Carly, give me a hand," Jim called out.

Billy Jo lifted the glass and took a swallow as the couple put the food on the table and the girls raced back in. He was getting the picture of a perfect family, and he could only imagine the questions Billy Jo had as one of the girls grabbed her hand and pulled her over to the bench to sit between them.

Yeah, now even he wanted to know what exactly had happened. Why had she abandoned her baby?

Chapter 12

She could hear Jim and the girls vaguely through the open upstairs window. Was he reading them a story or just getting them ready for bed? All she heard was laughter, still feeling the warmth that existed in this house, in this family. She should've been happy for the girls, but all it did was make the giant hole in her heart ache more than it had before she'd set foot on Carly Jackson's doorstep.

Now she sat in a big outdoor chair, Carly sitting across from her in the dark. The conversation piece was set well away from the house on the back lawn. This was the moment she'd waited all night for. She crossed her arms, feeling the chill and the buzz from the one glass of wine she'd had with dinner. Where was Mark? She didn't have a clue.

"So where do you want to start?" Carly said as she held another glass of wine and took yet another swallow. This was her third glass, and Billy Jo wondered whether it was liquid courage.

"How about the beginning, or how a meth addict goes

from that to this, or how you could just abandon me without a care in the world?"

For a second, she didn't answer. Then she said, "I was a stupid kid, is all. No excuses, but there is more to it. Not everything has a straightforward answer, Billy Jo." Carly shrugged, and for a moment, she thought her hand might have been shaking. She lifted the glass and took a drink. "I was a kid, had run away from home, gotten mixed up with the wrong crowd." She pulled in a breath and took another swallow.

Billy Jo wanted to yell at her to stop before she drank too much and wouldn't give her the answers she needed. It wasn't lost on her that Jim thought his wife was talking about Billy Jo's mother, who had been a friend of hers, a lost connection. It was laughable, if she thought about it.

Maybe she should start with the easier questions. "So how old were you?"

"Fifteen going on one step from the grave, a time of my life I wish I could forget."

Did she have any idea how much that comment hurt her? "I guess you won't be so lucky as to forget, because I'm very real, a living and breathing person, your daughter."

Carly lifted her gaze to Billy Jo, who realized she didn't understand how much she was hurting her. "Sorry?" There it was, the confusion in her blue eyes. There was so much about her face that was familiar. Anyone who really looked at them side by side could see they were related. "To be clear, you're not my daughter. You're just a baby I had."

The way she said that was like a slap to her face.

Billy Jo found herself gesturing vaguely. "Point taken. It was a bad choice of words. You're my birth mother, a fact you can't talk away from. You didn't want me, so you left me like I was garbage. Why? Before you go on, I get that you were fifteen, strung out on meth, a drug addict who couldn't have cared less about the baby she was carrying and how she was hurting it. Now here you are, with a family of your own, respectable—and a teacher, too. Did you ever spare me a passing thought? Ever wonder even a little about what could have happened to me?"

With a hard set of her jaw, Carly lifted her gaze to the second-story window, which was still open. She knew no one could hear them, because she could only just make out the voices of the girls and Jim.

"So you were fifteen," Billy Jo continued. "I was born in McDermitt, Nevada, but you're not from there?"

Carly blinked and pulled in a breath, sitting with a sweater pulled over her shoulders, her legs crossed. "I don't remember much. As I said, that was a bad time of my life. I'd hooked up with the wrong crowd. My mother died when I was thirteen, and my father didn't handle it well. He didn't notice when I disappeared with a group of kids who were struggling with their own issues at home. No one was happy. We skipped school, drank, partied. The drugs became an easy escape. I started with weed and easily moved on to other things. Not sure how meth became the drug of choice, but it did.

"My father figured out there was a problem when he had to bail me out of jail. By then I was pregnant, on a downward spiral. I had found myself in Carson City, not McDermitt, where you were born in the back of a brothel. I wasn't sure how the records about your birthplace would be handled. As a matter of fact, I vaguely remember having you. I never held you, because a baby like that wasn't expected to survive. I was sent to recovery, where I spent the next six months. I didn't expect you to land on my doorstep now. I was told you had been taken care of.

Whatever that meant, I didn't ask." She glanced away, and Billy Jo could feel the door shutting on her.

"I was born in Carson City?" she said. "But my birth certificate says—"

"Again, I have no idea what your birth certificate says, Billy Jo. All I know is that was a time of my life I'm trying to forget. Everything was taken care of: you, the paperwork, and me disappearing for a while. That wasn't me. That person doesn't exist. The only thing my husband knows is that I was messed up with drugs as a kid, but I got help and cleaned up my act. I'm sorry I can't help you, but I don't know what it is you're looking for. A happy ending? That's not going to happen. You said you have a mother and father, so good. I'm happy for you. Don't come in here, thinking there's going to be some reunion between you and me, because there won't be. There can't be." She was shaking her head, her voice so low and quiet that no one could overhear. "As far as my husband knows, I knew your mother. Let's keep it that way."

She sensed that only seconds remained before she would be asked to leave, and she had no answers. She could feel the hatred for her from someone who shouldn't despise her like this. Mothers were never supposed to hate their children.

"Do you have any idea what happens to a baby who's born to a meth addict?' she finally said.

Carly was stiff, tense, as she lifted her glass of wine and took another swallow. She glanced down and then looked away, and there it was: the guilt she hadn't thought she had. "If you're looking for an apology, there won't be one."

She just wasn't getting through to her. "I was a difficult baby to care for, in and out of the ER and hospital, a screamer. I was in agony, being weaned off the same drug you put into yourself. An unwanted baby, passed around from foster home to foster home. I may have a father and mother now, but at fifteen, I had been in too many foster homes to count, labeled difficult, troubled, damaged, abused, hurt. As a little kid, you learn early on that a safe place doesn't really exist. Do you want to know what happened to me, how old I was when I woke up with the son of one of my foster parents on top of me? It wasn't called rape, because no one I called would listen, seeing as my file already had me marked as a liar, a tramp, a whore who picked up men."

She expected remorse, something, but all Carly did was lift her glass, down the rest of the wine, and stand up. "Well, it's getting late," she said. "I'll see you out."

So that was it. Uncared for, unwanted.

"Who was my father?"

Carly stilled where she stood with her back to Billy Jo. Then she turned, not looking right at her, and shook her head. Just then, she spotted the back French doors opening. Mark and Jim were talking, both walking out of the house, coming their way.

"As I said to you, I was messed up and did things I don't even remember," Carly said. "I have no answer to give you. I don't know. Please, I've told you all I can…"

"Hey, you two, are you all caught up?" Jim slid his arm around Carly and kissed her head, and Billy Jo knew she wasn't going to get anything else.

"Yeah," Carly said. "I told her what I could remember, but it was a long time ago. As I said to Billy Jo, I'm remembering someone who isn't around anymore. So are the girls asleep?"

There it was, the change in subject.

"Tucked in, not quite asleep," Jim said.

"Well, I'll go up and check in a minute. Billy Jo was just saying she has to get going. I'll walk you out," Carly said.

Billy Jo knew she wasn't telling her the whole truth or any part of it as she dragged her hardened gaze between her and Mark.

"Thanks again for dinner," Mark said, jumping in. "Ready?"

All she wanted to do was yell and scream and say no, but she said, "Sure."

Carly handed Jim her empty wine glass and started walking back to the house. Billy Jo and Mark fell in behind her.

"You have everything?" Carly said. "You leave a purse or anything inside?"

"No, I have everything," she said. Her purse was in the car, and her keys were in her pocket. She could feel the rush to get her out of there.

She followed Carly to a side gate, which led back around the front, realizing Jim hadn't followed them as they walked to the driveway, past the BMW. She could just make out her small car parked in the dark on the road.

"Well, again, goodnight," was all Carly said, her arms pulled around her, the beautiful house she lived in behind her.

"You didn't answer all my questions," Billy Jo said, knowing Mark was right there, saying nothing but hearing everything.

"I gave all the answers I can, so please don't come back," Carly said. She nodded toward Billy Jo's car and took a step back.

Billy Jo felt Mark's hand on her arm. She wanted to make Carly tell her the truth, tell her more, tell her everything she was hiding.

"Billy Jo, let's go," he prompted, and she knew she couldn't push any more, not tonight.

"Fine. But I know you're hiding something, Carly. I'll leave, but you and I, we're far from done."

Carly's expression suddenly turned ugly, and Mark had her turned and walking to her car.

"Keep walking," he ordered. "Get in. Drive."

As she climbed in the vehicle, Mark closed the passenger door, and she started up the car and watched Carly go back inside, close the front door behind her, and turn off the outside light. She realized that if she were smart, she'd let all of this go.

"She's lying, Mark."

He gestured toward the house. "I know, but you may want to ask yourself why. She has secrets. Everyone does."

She put the car in gear and pulled away from the house after switching on her headlights. "So is this where you tell me to leave it alone, leave her alone?" She flicked her signal light at the end of the street and slowed.

"You can push and dig, but at which point are you hurting yourself more by trying to find out which secrets she's hiding? Sometimes things are best left where they are. You may not want to know, Billy Jo."

She gave the car gas and turned onto another darkened road that led into town. "Is that what you would do, Mark, if you were me?"

He was sitting so quietly in the passenger side as she waited, wondering what he'd heard, what he knew. So much about him was a mystery. "If it were me, I don't know how I'd feel. But it's not me. Unfortunately, sometimes, when you dig and dig and uncover the skeletons someone has buried, you wish you hadn't. Is it easier not knowing? Absolutely, just like burying your head in the sand."

"Is that a yes or no?" she snapped.

He chuckled softly under his breath. "I suppose I'd be a

dog with a bone too, Billy Jo. I wouldn't stop until I uncovered every dark, dirty thing. But again, that's just me. This is you and your life. You need to decide what you can live with, what you can know and still be able to sleep at night. That's all I'm saying. This is your decision. Just be careful how much you push for, and tread carefully."

She heard the warning and knew what she needed to do. "Thanks, Mark."

"For what?" he said. She could feel him watching her as she drove, seeing the lights of downtown and the sheriff's office, where his Jeep was parked.

"For not telling me to back off. For tagging along," she said.

And for making her feel, for the first time in her life, that she wasn't being completely ridiculous for wanting to know all about who she was, wanting to fill the missing hole of what had happened to baby Billy Jo Thornton, who had been dumped into a system that had shaped everything she was today.

"You're welcome," he said.

Chapter 13

Billy Jo slid her bag over her shoulder and closed her car door. The lights were out at Lorne and Lesley Lancaster's house, leaving her standing in total darkness on the isolated property. As she looked around, she had the odd sense that anything could happen, and it had the hairs on the back of her neck standing up.

She pulled out her cell phone and flicked the flashlight on to shine it at her darkened stairs. Since she had planned to come back and change before dinner, she hadn't left her outside light on that morning. She climbed the steps, fighting the urge to look back.

When had the detective changed from a pain in the ass, an arrogant jerk, to a man who was so damn supportive of her for reasons she couldn't figure out? Then there was Carly, who had made her feel so vile and dirty. She thought also about the case of the young woman, Brenda, who had shown far more restraint than she ever would have.

Today had sucked, frankly.

She turned the doorknob, but it didn't give, because it was locked. She let out a sigh of relief. Mark's comment about her unlocked door had made her lock it behind her that morning. She slid her key in, opened it, and stepped in, hearing a meow before she flicked on the light.

Her cell phone started ringing. She closed the door and took in Harley hopping her way as she set her bag down on the floor. Her cell phone displayed a private number, so it could be anyone. Right now, she just wanted a bath, and she figured if it was that important, the call wouldn't be coming from a blocked number. She pressed decline and tossed her cell phone on the island before reaching down to lift Harley.

"I'm so sorry you were left alone all day," she said, listening to him purr as she snuggled him. His bowl was half full of dry food, and the water dish needed to be refreshed.

The clock on the stove showed it was close to ten. She should've been tired, but she was too worked up. She put the cat down and changed his water, then walked over to her bag and pulled out her laptop and the file. As she set them on the small table in the living room, she thought of what to put in the report.

She strode into the bathroom, put the stopper in the bathtub, and turned on the tap. A bath would settle her, then some comfortable pajamas, and she would tackle that report before tomorrow arrived, far too soon.

Her cell phone started ringing again.

She left the bathroom and took in the same private number on the screen before picking it up. She hesitated only a second before answering it. "Hello?"

No one said anything.

"Who is this? Is anyone there? Hello…?"

There was static. She waited another second before pulling the phone away from her ear. The click from the other end told her they had hung up.

Then her phone dinged with a message: a photo of her leaving her office earlier. She took in her distracted look, her bag over her shoulder as she walked to her car. What the hell? Her stomach bottomed out, and she shot a glance at the door, seeing it was still unlocked. Her heart thudded as she moved to it, her hand shaking as she turned the deadbolt.

She stared at the door, then at her phone again, at the photo from the unknown number.

Was this a joke? She thumbed through the message and typed a text: *Who is this? What do you want?*

She waited, but there was nothing, no reply.

Seriously, are you watching me? Who are you?

She could hear her bathtub still running, and she started back to the bathroom. It was almost full, steaming. She turned it off, hearing the ding of a new text.

It was another photo from the same unknown number, and she had to remind herself to breathe. It was a photo of her place, taken from outside the window. Her cat, Harley, was sleeping on the sofa.

But there was no text to follow, no other response. She listened to the quiet of the night and watched her cat hop into the living room, feeling the fear that someone she didn't know was trying to scare the hell out of her.

She sent another text back: *Look, I'm going to call the cops on you. Who is this?*

Her heart was thumping, and her palms were sweating as she pressed a hand to her forehead. No response.

Leave me alone! she texted, then put her phone down on the island.

She just took in her empty place, feeling the isolation, the kind of fear she hadn't felt in a long time. She snatched her phone back up and scrolled to Mark's number, then hesitated, feeling foolish for a second as her thumb hovered over the call button. She shouldn't. It was late. He'd think she was crazy.

"Fuck, just do it, already!" she muttered.

She could feel the ache in her chest from the building anxiety as she pressed the call button and put the phone to her ear, wrapping her other arm around her waist and holding it there, listening to the ring.

"Yeah, what?" There it was, the rudeness, the arrogance she expected.

"Detective, it's Billy Jo. Listen, I know this may sound odd, but I think someone is watching me."

She wasn't sure what she heard in the background.

"What do you mean, someone is watching you? You see something? You see someone?"

She shook her head and realized it sounded more like a prank than anything, nothing anyone could do anything about. "No, nothing like that. Someone called me just now as I was getting home, an unknown number. They texted me two photos, one of me coming out of my office today and one of my place, of my cat, taken from outside my window. I've texted them back, demanding to know who it is, but they're not responding. The number is blocked, private."

He said nothing for a second, then, "And nothing else, no messages, just the photos?" She shut her eyes and tilted her head back, hearing something in the background again. She realized it was a woman. Now she felt like an absolute idiot.

"You want me to come over, have a look around?"

"You know what? Forget it. I think after tonight, today, I'm just overreacting. My door's locked. Just forget I called."

Yeah, there was definitely a woman there with him, and she didn't know why that bothered her. A guy like him, who looked like him, of course he had a woman there. She knew that arrogant alpha persona was a magnet for women.

"You sure I can't come over, have a look around?"

She was already shaking her head even though he couldn't see her. "No, I'm fine. Sorry to call and bother you."

"Listen, forward me the photos. And if you get any more, let me know."

She pulled the phone away from her ear after saying goodbye and hung up, feeling stupid as she forwarded the photos to Mark.

The text back from him was immediate: *Creepy! I'll check into it. Call me if you get any more. Lock your door!*

She pulled in a breath. She didn't know why, but despite how silly she felt, someone knowing about this made her feel better.

She took in her cat, who was settling in on the sofa, and remembered her bath. Then she looked over to the kitchen table and the two chairs sitting there. She lifted one and carried it to the door, where she propped it under the door handle. No one was going to get inside her apartment.

She'd have a bath, put on her pajamas, type up the report, and watch the door until the sun came up. And then, tomorrow, she could figure out who was trying to freak her out.

Chapter 14

"Just dropping me off here is fine. Thanks for a fun night," Sybil said as she leaned across his Jeep and offered her lips, the same ones that had been his distraction.

When Billy Jo dropped him off at the station the night before, Sybil had just been leaving the coffee house nearby, and she had stopped in front of his Jeep and suggested sex. What was he supposed to have said? He still laughed, thinking of her bold move.

"Anytime," he said. "Have a great day." He made a point of not kissing her lips, instead pressing a kiss to her forehead, then gestured to the coffeeshop he was idling in front of. He didn't want their night together morphing into anything serious, but she was gorgeous and leggy and had provided a welcome distraction.

She climbed out and said, "Do you want to come in for coffee?"

He was already shaking his head, his hand resting on the gearshift. "Can't. Got a meeting. Have to get to it." He knew how to make sure the door was closed and no ideas of happily ever after were lingering in her mind.

She shrugged. "Okay. See you when I see you," she said. Then she closed the door.

He had to chuckle under his breath, thinking of how unshy she'd been the night before. From the back seat, the dog leaned forward to lick his face, and Mark groaned to him. "Hey, knock it off! So you had to sleep on the floor. You're a dog. It's not the end of the world."

He pulled away and drove the block to the sheriff's office, seeing the chief's truck and Carmen's cruiser there. So he wasn't the first in. He parked beside the cruiser, and the dog followed him in and ran over to the dog bed Gail had insisted on buying. He settled in, and Mark took in Carmen over by the coffeepot. The chief's office door was closed, and he was on the phone.

"Chief's here early, I see," Mark said. "So what's up today?"

Carmen poured a coffee, not turning as she said, "He was here before me. He's been in his office on the phone the entire time except for the few minutes when he told me to make coffee and bring him one." She held up the mug as if showing him. So that was why she had an odd look on her face.

She tapped on the chief's door, then opened it when he didn't answer and stepped inside. Mark watched him pull the phone away from his mouth and say, "Thank you. Make sure the weekly report is on my desk by end of day."

It wasn't lost on him that the chief had only ever asked Carmen to get him a coffee. Never once had he asked Mark. He wondered what she really thought, as she had never said that it bothered her. She closed the door again as she walked out, and Mark poured a coffee and held it out to her as she walked his way. She took it with surprise.

"The Chief's in a mood," she said. "He wants the weekly report early, the one on all the incidents on the island. I don't usually submit it until Thursday, but for some reason he wants it today."

Mark reached for another mug and poured himself a coffee as Carmen dumped some sugar in hers. "Any idea who he's talking to?"

She only shrugged. "Nope. Didn't ask, either. Not my business. Seems to have talked to a few people already."

He wondered at times how she could do that. "Listen, you know anyone who can trace a private blocked cell phone number—quietly?"

She looked up at him. "So you have a number, and you need to find out who it is?"

"Yeah, and discreetly, too."

"So unofficially, then." She stirred her coffee, then tapped the spoon on the edge of the mug and put it on the counter.

"If at all possible."

"You want to provide me anything else? Is this part of a case, personal…?"

"How about you get me the details of who it is, and then I can figure out from there whether it becomes official?"

She shrugged again and said, "Send it to me."

There was just something about Carmen that he liked, but she held her cards closer than anyone he'd ever met. What was it about this island? It seemed to be a hotbed of secrets.

He pulled out his phone and forwarded Carmen the text Billy Jo had sent him the night before with the photo of her cat.

Carmen looked at her cell phone. "Should I ask?" was all she said.

He just shook his head. "No, just tell me who it is—and the address too, please."

She shook her head, then glanced to the chief's office as the door was yanked open.

"Mark, get in here," the chief said.

Mark turned to him, remembering well what the chief had said to him the morning before, showing up at his place. He took his coffee with him and shoved his cell phone in the pocket of his blue jeans as he stepped into the chief's office.

The chief stepped back around the desk and sat in his overstuffed black chair. "Close the door," he said, gesturing toward it. He really was in a mood this morning, and Mark wondered what he was in for.

He closed the door.

"Dinner at the Jacksons' last night," the chief said, "how did it go?"

What was it about the way he asked? He realized this wasn't a friendly morning chat. He'd never been able to find out anything about the chief and Jim other than that they'd grown up together and were friends.

"Great," he said. "But I don't think you called me into your office for a friendly chat about the dinner I had with a friend of yours last night. So I'll get right to it: It was a nice dinner. We had meatloaf, which was the best I've ever had, though I'll deny that if anyone tells my mother. We talked about nothing important—the island, the locals, and life here. Carly and Billy Jo had a chance to catch up alone outside after dinner. What they talked about, I have no idea, because I stayed inside with your friend, who seemed to know a lot about who had the job here before me. Jim's father is a partner in SJ Holdings, one of the big resort developers this side of the Pacific. It was friendly, and that was how we left last night, on friendly terms."

The chief leaned back in his chair without pulling his gaze. "Yes, I already know that part. I spoke with Jim already. We had quite the talk about you. He likes you. Ms. McCabe is kind of an unknown, though. Not really sure what to make of her. You see, the thing about unknowns is that they're wildcards, which can be dangerous. Apparently, Carly is still claiming Billy Jo is the daughter of an old friend, a teenage meth addict. However, the birth certificate for Billy Jo Thornton has the mother listed as Carly Thornton, father unknown." The chief put both feet on the ground.

He knew.

"You're a good detective, Mark, but you're not the best. I see you didn't think I'd find out. Told you, when I ask you to tell me everything, I expect everything. Don't pull this bullshit. Why you're protecting Ms. McCabe, I'll never know, but your loyalty is here." The chief had a way of looking at him that was damn unnerving. "Did my own digging into the girl. Imagine my surprise to learn that Carly Jackson used to be Carly Thornton. But I'm pretty sure you already knew that."

He made himself pull in a breath, holding his steaming coffee, knowing he needed to be really careful of what he said next. "If you know, why are you asking me?" he said. "I think you can understand now why Billy Jo showed up. She has questions. She wants answers. I suppose Jim knows now, too. So I guess all this is a moot point."

The chief said nothing for a second. Something in his expression softened. "Far be it from me to fill Jim in on Carly's past, who she was. She hid it from him. Not sure why, but I'm not about to tell him. So Ms. McCabe knows now. Can we agree this is the end of it? There will be no more showing up on the Jacksons' doorstep. She's to let it go, and I mean everything. Carly seems to have a lot of skeletons in her closet. That would be a problem if Jim were running for public office, but he's not."

Mark wondered what the chief knew that he didn't. He thought of the texts last night and how Carly hadn't really given Billy Jo all the answers she needed. "Then I'm not sure what else you need from me," he said. He knew he should be careful, but there was just something about this man, his boss. Somehow, he didn't think this was the end of it.

"What I expect, Mark, is for there to be no problems here. I can tell Jim this is the end of it, and Carly gets to keep her secret. Pretty sure this would be what makes everyone happy, don't you think? A teenage girl who screwed up is allowed to get a second chance. Hell, look at Ms. McCabe and the trouble she created for herself. She got a second chance with a nice family, and she's defied the odds for a kid in the foster system, in jail, or on the streets. She's actually almost respectable. What do you say this thing goes away?"

It took Mark another second to understand his meaning. "I can't speak for Billy Jo, Chief. I'm not going to tell her to stop digging. So I guess you can tell Jim Jackson whatever you want. This isn't a police matter. It's something between Billy Jo and Carly."

The chief leaned forward and rested his forearms on his desk. "Well, then I guess we'd have a problem. If I were you, Mark, I'd explain to Ms. McCabe how unhealthy it is for her to go digging around in something that isn't her business. Do we understand each other?" The way the chief said it gave Mark a feeling this was going nowhere good.

"Clearly," was all he said as he reached for the door and pulled it open.

"Good. Glad we cleared this up. Listen, Gail won't be

back until tomorrow, so I need you to man the phones again. Close the door on your way out."

As Mark stepped out of the chief's office and pulled the door closed behind him, he heard the ding of his phone. At his desk, he saw the message from Carmen.

Got something on that number. See attached. And just FYI, you didn't get this from me.

He looked over to Carmen's empty desk, wondering how the hell she'd managed to disappear so quietly. He glanced back to the chief in his office on the phone again before opening the attachment. The name he didn't recognize, but the address he did.

All he could think was that he needed to talk to Billy Jo right now.

Chapter 15

Her report was done, filed, and all Grant had replied via email was *Great. Follow up. That is all.*

It was that last sentence that bothered her, because it meant Brenda and her husband's lives had been turned upside down and a report created, a black mark against her, only for the incident to be filed away now.

Then there was Pam, who'd been avoiding her all morning, on the phone or running errands. Billy Jo sat on her side of the cubicle, listening for the moment she hung up the phone. She strode around before Pam could get up or pick up the phone again, and she took in her wide eyes at her undoubtedly pissed-off expression.

"So, about Ms. Burns," Billy Jo said. "You know, the complaint you forwarded to Grant? Do you want to explain how a complaint from Cecily Tucker made its way in here, considering it was based on a dream she had? I have to wonder. You've been living here a really long time and have worked here for ten years, so you must know most of the people on the island. Their baby was injured during delivery because of a doctor error, yet Brenda is dealing with it well. I took the detective with me to investigate this troubling claim, by the way, and he had a word with Ms. Tucker, in case you're wondering, to make it clear to her that dreams are not reality. Do you care to explain to me how the complaint was filed? Because I'm pretty sure more questions should have been asked."

Pam's expression told her how uncomfortable she was. It appeared she was already aware of what had happened, and she gestured vaguely.

Billy Jo made no move to leave. In fact, she crossed her arms. "Not going to answer, really? An official complaint based on a dream. You know that's a black mark in Brenda Burns' file now. You think she deserves that? I'm required to go back again even though the complaint isn't valid, because logic really doesn't come into play sometimes in this system. But you can be damn sure I'll see to it that Brenda gets every and any service available for her son."

She wondered what she was seeing in Pam's expression as the woman said, "Look, I didn't know for sure. If I hadn't filed the complaint and something had happened, it would tie up this office in a shitstorm. My motto is that when a complaint comes in, you check it out. A dream? Well, I'm sure Cecily had it because she fears something could happen."

What was really going through her mind? Billy Jo wondered. "Do you have issues with Brenda Burns? Do you know her?"

Pam leaned back in her chair, lifting her hands in defense. "Only what Cecily has said about her. When Trent took up with her, she said she'd ruin him. I know that's not enough of a reason, but Brenda drove a wedge between Cecily and Trent. They were always close. Then Brenda entered the picture, and—"

"You know what this sounds like, Pam?" she said,

cutting her off. Billy Jo was pissed and tired, having spent the night on the sofa, staring at the door, after finishing the report. She had woken after a few hours' sleep to the sun streaming through the window and her cat on top of her. "It sounds like a mother-in-law who hates the girl her son took up with. Vengeful, spiteful, angry… Any of those words ring a bell to you? You seriously wasted time and energy on this crazy lady and didn't shut her down? A dream! I've never heard anything as crazy as that. Don't do it again, Pam. You know the people on this island and who Cecily is. This shouldn't have happened."

She knew it had come out quite sharply, and she expected Pam to say something else, to come back with another comment about the situation, the family, but instead all she did was lift her hands and say, "Point taken, but we've always done things a certain way on the island."

Whatever that meant, she wasn't sure she wanted to know. At least now she knew that she and Pam would never be friends.

She heard her cell phone ringing, so she walked away, back to her cubby, seeing the detective's name on the screen just as it went to voicemail. She didn't know why she had hesitated. Maybe she remembered too well the woman's voice she'd heard in the background the night before.

She took in the time and knew she had a list of foster kids to follow up on, homes she should drop in on. The agency didn't allow spot checks, but she wondered, could she have been protected any better if they had?

"Pam, I'm heading out," she said. "If anyone calls the office, have them call my cell."

Pam was now at the copier but turned her way. "Sure," was all she said.

Billy Jo lifted her bag and put it over her shoulder, seeing the voicemail. She'd listen on the way.

As she thought about it now, maybe her call to Mark had been an overreaction. At the same time, as she walked out the front door and locked it behind her, she found herself looking up and around, wondering if someone was watching.

She headed to her car, climbed behind the wheel, and started the engine, thinking of the woman who hadn't given her all the answers she wanted. She turned left and started down the main busy road, past the ferry traffic into town, when her cell phone started ringing again.

She reached into her bag on the passenger seat and pulled it out, then rested it on the console between the seats. She really needed to get Bluetooth set up in her car. She pressed the green answer button, seeing it was the detective again.

"I'm just driving to a meeting," she said. "Can I call you back?"

"Where are you?" he said, almost cutting her off.

She left the downtown area and followed the narrow road as it curved. "Just outside town, heading to Rourke Road. Why, what's wrong?"

"I had someone do some digging about the number that texted you those photos last night. Someone was watching you at your house. I found out who it is."

She found herself really listening to him as she drove around the bend, the road becoming narrow, trees on both sides. She hit a rut and put her foot on the brake to slow down, then felt the wobble of her wheel. *What the hell?*

"What's wrong?" he said.

She hadn't realized she'd said it out loud. "I don't know. My wheel's wobbling..." She had to really grip the steering wheel as she pushed the brake and moved to gear down.

"Pull over," he said. "I'll come out there now. We need to talk."

She saw the bend just as she pressed the brake, the car wobbling, heading closer to the steep ditch over the bank. *Damn, damn, damn...*

She could hear Mark yelling on the other end as she fought to hold the car steady. It swerved, and she felt the clunk, jolted by a hard crash, the sound of metal grinding. A tree was coming right at her. She felt the hard stop, the explosion of the airbag, then nothing but a hiss and ringing in her ears.

"BILLY JO!" Mark called, running from his Jeep. He had started driving, having an idea where she was, and had heard the crash. When she didn't answer, he feared the worst. Her car was on its side in the steep ditch, and a wheel had fallen off. He could hear the sirens in the distance as he slid on the car, looking through the passenger window. He didn't see any movement. One of the airbags had deployed.

"Billy Jo, it's Mark. Answer me. Are you okay? I called for help. An ambulance is on its way. Don't look up here! I'm going to break the glass."

He thought he heard her groan, and he reached into his jacket and pulled out a pocketknife. He pressed the straight edge of the tool to the closed passenger window, and it shattered. Glass was everywhere. He could see her hand move, pressing at the airbag.

"You okay? Are you hurt?" He hung his head in.

She brushed the shower of glass pellets away from her

face. There was a trickle of blood at her hairline and another on her hand. "I'm fine, just pissed. My wheel fell off. Get me out of here."

Mark climbed in through the window and stepped on the console, then used his pocketknife to poke the airbag. Her seatbelt was still on. He could see that she may have hit her head. She reached for the seatbelt and unhooked it, seeming a little disoriented.

"How about we wait for the paramedics to get you out?" he said. "You may have a neck injury. Let's get a collar on you, at least."

But she was already shaking her head, climbing around to get up.

He could hear that the ambulance was already there. "All right, easy does it. Take my hand. I'll help you up."

The car was still in the ditch, at an angle, and a head poked in the passenger window. It was JC, one of the full-time paramedics on the island, with light hair and freckles. He maneuvered around the door and held out his hand.

Mark put his hand on Billy Jo's waist and called out, "I'll lift her up! Billy Jo, reach up and take JC's hand."

He lifted her, and JC pulled, and Billy Jo was out. He heard the paramedics talking to her as he pulled himself out, taking in the mangled car, which was likely beyond repair. Billy Jo was sitting at the back of the ambulance, its lights flashing.

He jumped to the ground and wiped the shards of glass from his pants. Seeing the wheel on the road, he knew how much worse it could've been. He looked right and left and pulled in a breath, then ran his hand over his face as he walked over to the ambulance.

The paramedics were doing triage, applying a white bandage to her head and checking her eyes for a head injury.

"Mark, my car…" she said.

He just shook his head. "It's a write-off. You were lucky —it could've been worse." He turned to Deanna, the other paramedic, with short dark hair, who was taping the gauze to Billy Jo's forehead. "You're taking her to the hospital?"

"Yeah, to check her out," she said.

"I'm fine," Billy Jo said. "I don't need to go to the hospital."

He sensed she was ready to argue, and he took in the paramedic, who would likely let her go. "Can you give us a second?" he said.

Deanna pulled off her rubber gloves. "Sure," she said.

Mark watched the paramedic climb into the ambulance and took in Billy Jo, who seemed to make nothing easy. As she glanced up at him, he could see the rattled look, and he wondered what to say. "You okay? Really?"

She seemed to slouch for a minute, then shrugged. "I don't know. It's been a really trying last few days, and now this?" She gestured toward the car. He knew what she meant. "I'm almost afraid to ask, but you said you found out who was sending the texts to me. I know this may sound paranoid, but I can't help thinking this has to do with Carly."

As he looked over to the car on its side in the ditch, its wheel lying in the road, he couldn't help the wave of fear that hit him. This seemed so much like a message. "We traced it back to someone by the name of Clifton Harris. I didn't place the name at first, but I recognized the address. It's above the main post office in town."

Billy Jo was giving him everything, and he wasn't sure what to make of the question in her eyes.

"It likely was Carly or Jim," he said. "They hired someone. Clifton Harris is the alias of a local PI. His hourly rate has him doing the kinds of things that get results for people who can afford him. Carmen was on her way over to see him when I called you."

As she sat there on the back of that ambulance, he wasn't sure she believed him. "So now what?" she said.

He just shook his head. "We'll bring him in, have a talk with him, and make it clear that we know it was him. Then he'll tell his clients. Billy Jo, you may want to ask yourself something about Carly and Jim. I know you want more answers, but they've come out swinging. They could try to hurt you or scare you off, which I'm pretty sure they were trying to do with those texts."

She breathed in and out.

"Excuse me, Detective, but we need to go," JC said, striding around the ambulance to him.

Mark only nodded and said, "Well?"

He could see Billy Jo was having some trouble before she nodded and said, "Fine. Let's go." As she stood up, he could see the scratches, the marks on her bare arms. She glanced over to him. "You want me to drop it, don't you?"

He wondered whether she'd listen. "I want you to be okay with what you already know."

She only nodded, then rested her hand on the back door of the ambulance. "You know what? I am okay with everything she said. It's not what I wanted, but then, I don't know what I wanted."

He watched as JC helped her in and she sat on the bench on the side. His hand was still on the door as he said, "Oh, I think you, more than anyone, know exactly what you want."

He thought she smiled. Then she winced. "You're right. I do," she said. "And, Mark, in case I didn't say it, thanks."

He just shrugged and reached for the door, ready to close it. "Anytime, Billy Jo. Anytime."

Chapter 16

For a small island hospital, the emergency room was busy. It seemed accidents and emergencies happened here, too.

Billy Jo took in the blue curtains of her exam room, hearing a man snoring softly from the one beside her. The old doctor putting in stitches at her hairline was wearing reading glasses, which didn't give her the confidence in his skill she'd have preferred.

She had seen Mark a moment ago just outside the curtained-off area, talking to the chief, another man she had never seen before, and a woman she thought was Carly Jackson. But that was impossible. Maybe she'd hit her head harder than she realized.

"Your sure you can see?" Billy Jo said. "Exactly how old are you, again?"

The doctor smiled, and his hazel eyes flicked down to her as he held the needle with the scissors and snipped. He wore a white dress shirt and tie, dressed like a businessman rather than a doctor, which was freaking her out more.

"Now, don't you worry none about my eyesight," he

said. "These reading glasses let me see everything, and I've been doing this since long before you were born. Why, I could do this with my eyes closed."

"Please don't," she said, and even she could hear the panic in her voice.

The doctor chuckled under his breath. "Almost there. Last one. Hold still." He snipped again.

She relaxed her hands, which had fisted the sheet covering the gurney beneath her, as she let out a breath. She hadn't expected an old guy like that to be able to put in stitches without leaving her looking like a freak.

He held up a mirror to her, and she took in the dried blood, the swelling, and the three stitches as he said, "See? There it is. Looks pretty damn good." Then he taped a bandage over the stitches, pulled off his latex gloves, and stood and smiled down at her. "You'll be just fine. I have to say, that's the best work I've ever done. You likely won't even have a scar. You're all set. Remember, you have a mild concussion, so have someone at home to keep an eye on you. Any dizziness, vomiting…"

Mark, who still had his detective badge attached to his belt, was standing in the opening of the curtain, taking her in. "Is she ready to go?"

"All done," the doctor said. "And you remember what I told you: Keep an eye out, and take a couple days off to take it easy. No driving, too. Those are the doctor's orders."

"Thanks, Doc," Mark said, then patted the old doctor's back before he strode out.

Billy Jo swung her legs over the side of the gurney, feeling the stiffness setting in everywhere.

"You ready?" Mark said.

She looked up and over to him, feeling the tightness in her neck, though her headache was now fading from the

Tylenol. "Yup. Oh, shoot. I should call in to the office. My phone, my bag…"

"I already called. Got your things from your car, too—which I also want to talk about."

The curtain on the other side of the room was brushed back to reveal the chief, such a big man. Behind him was the other man she didn't recognize.

"Hey there, young lady. You sure worried some folks," Chief Shepard said. There was something about the way the chief spoke at times that had her wanting to snarl back at him and remind him she had a name. "This is Russ Marshall."

She stared at the man. Dark hair and beard, a few inches shorter than Mark, with a solid build. His eyes, she figured, were a cross between vivid blue and green against his brown skin. His lips were full.

He didn't pull his gaze from her as he held out his hand. "Good to meet you, Billy Jo, although I wish circumstances were better."

"Sure, but who are you?" she said, staying where she was. His handshake was firm. She found herself looking over to Mark, and no one said anything for a second.

"Russ is the PI I was telling you about," Mark said, "the one who goes by Clifton Harris. It's an alias he's used at times."

She wasn't sure she'd heard him correctly.

Russ made an odd face, likely about the name. "As I said to the chief, it's one of many names I use when working a case. It just comes with the job."

"I'm sorry," Billy Jo said, "but did you just say you're the person who sent me those texts last night to basically terrorize me? What is this? You want to show up and say it in person? Were you really hired by Carly and Jim?" She dragged her gaze back to Mark, who only shook his head.

"Look, I've already said this to the chief and to the deputy who showed up at my place earlier," Russ replied. "That was one of my phones, but it wasn't me. The phone was stolen. To be frank, as I also pointed out, sending photos to scare someone isn't my style."

She wasn't sure what to make of that. The chief hadn't pulled his gaze from the man, whereas Mark glanced to the ceiling, as if he had more to say or knew something else. Maybe if her head didn't still hurt, she'd be able to think clearer and it wouldn't seem so confusing.

"So what is this, then?" Billy Jo said. "Some sicko is still out there. One of those photos was taken outside my place, looking through my window at my cat. You already said Jim and Carly—"

"It wasn't either of them," the chief said, cutting in. "Russ works for lots of folks, and he's here now voluntarily to straighten this out. So are the Jacksons."

All she could do was stare and wonder what else was coming her way.

"Then there's the matter of your car," Mark said. "Your wheel falling off wasn't just bad maintenance. It had us taking another look, and we've just heard back that the wheel was tampered with. That kind of changes the look of this. Someone made sure it was loose enough to fall off. It could've been worse, could've killed you or someone else on the road. That changes the entire investigation."

Again, she stared. "So would the person who tampered with my wheel be the same one who sent me photos from Russ's stolen phone? Seems rather convenient, if you ask me." She gestured toward the PI, whom she wasn't sure she trusted.

He only shrugged. The way his hard gaze lingered, she had the feeling he had secrets he wouldn't tell anyone. "Sometimes the truth really is that simple," he said. "As

I've already told the chief, I have a lot of burners, a lot of phones. It's the business I'm in. They get lost, stolen. It happens. Not a big deal. I've offered to help find out who it is."

She found herself looking at the chief and then Mark, wondering if they had swallowed that line, because even to her, it sounded like someone covering his ass.

"It seems that's our best lead," the chief said. "In the meantime, evidently, someone is upset with you. Since you can't go home until we find out who this person is, do you have someone you can stay with?"

Her jaw slackened. There was a feeling she couldn't shake about the chief, as if every time he spoke, he was trying to point the finger at her, as if she were responsible for everything that had befallen her. "No, I don't have someone to stay with, but I'm sure if I tell my landlords, Lesley and Lorne, they'll keep an eye out."

"She can stay with me," Mark said.

Just then, a nurse appeared behind the chief and said something to him.

"Excuse me," the chief told them. Then he and the PI stepped out.

Billy Jo stared at Mark. "I'm not staying with you, Detective, although I appreciate it. I would prefer just to go home."

He took a step closer to her. She could hear other voices out there and thought of the work she needed to do, the meeting she'd missed. She wanted to lie down for a bit. How could Jim and Carly be there now, too? This didn't seem real.

"You can't, Billy Jo. Not until we find out who's coming after you. The wheel on your car not being an accident changes things. This isn't someone trying to scare you; this is someone trying to hurt you, maybe kill you. The chief is right about that much."

She knew what he was saying. "Are you sure it's not that PI, Russ? Because that story of his sounds like bullshit. You told me it was Jim and Carly, it had to be. Are you now saying it's not?"

"I'm not often wrong, Billy Jo, but you should know Carly is here, just like the chief said. And she wants to talk to you."

From behind Mark came voices and footsteps, and then Carly appeared.

"Hi," she said. "So how are you doing?"

For a moment, Billy Jo just stared, wondering again whether she had hit her head harder than she thought. Then she said, "Stitches, as you can see. A little stiff, but I'm fine. Why are you here? Because if I recall, after last night, you wanted nothing to do with me. In fact, up until a second ago, it seemed you were trying to scare me off, scare me away. I was told you and your husband were behind this."

There was something about the way Carly was looking at her. Her expression no longer held the horror that had been there, as if Billy Jo held the bomb that would destroy her life. She seemed far too calm and in control now. She glanced over to Mark. "Detective, could you give us a moment?"

Mark lingered for a second. "Billy Jo, you okay with this?"

She just lifted her hand impatiently, abruptly, rudely. "It's fine."

He stepped out.

Carly reached for the one curtain and pulled it closed. It provided a measure of privacy, but that was it. "Tolly called me after your accident and told me about you being harassed. He asked me outright if Russ was working for me or Jim. I'm telling you, that phone call was enough for my husband to pull me aside, sit me down, and ask what the hell was going on. He knew I was lying about something. It's just something you know when you're married to someone. You figure out pretty quick who your partner is. I knew my time was up. I was terrified, but I had to tell him."

Billy Jo just stared at her, wondering if this was where she would say she was sorry. But as soon as the thought came, she realized an apology was likely never coming. "So you told him about me?"

Carly's hands were shoved in the pockets of her navy blue fall coat. Her dark hair was brushed straight. She had that same haunted look on her face. She nodded. "I told my husband everything. It was one of the most difficult talks I've ever had. I expected him to hate me, but he doesn't. He was furious, let me tell you, for my never having told him to begin with about what happened to me. Honestly, Billy Jo, the truth is that I wish you never showed up on my doorstep, but you did. Now here you are in the hospital, hurt, almost killed, and the spotlight was shining on me and my husband. I can't have that. But now I need to say that I never told you everything."

Billy Jo's hands curled around the sheets where she was sitting. "I know you didn't," she said. "I'm not a fool. I know when someone is lying or has spun a situation and expects me to just swallow it. How much of the version you told me is the truth? The fact that you just walked away…"

Carly glanced at the curtain, her arms pulled tight around herself. "Yes, my husband said the same thing, but I'll tell you that walking away was the kindest thing I could have done for you. As you said, I was an addict whose only want was my next fix. Thinking back to that time, it was a blur. The fact was that I was trying to drown out the image of him, your father, but just looking at you now, I can see his face as if it were yesterday."

She paced there in front of her, blowing out a breath, having trouble speaking, and for a moment, Billy Jo was too stunned to say a word.

"Do you know what I remember?" Carly continued. "I told you about the trouble I got into as a kid, the drugs, but what I didn't tell you was what drove me there to begin with. He was a man who was old enough to be my father, a man my father introduced me to, someone he did business with. One day, he took me out for coffee. Oh, he was very good looking, and I was an infatuated kid. He drove me to his place and held me down in his garage, and he raped me not just once but over and over for two days. Then he made me clean up and drove me back.

"My father was home. He had never even realized I was gone. I went up to my room, and the man who'd brutalized me was downstairs with my father, having drinks, laughing." She pulled in a breath. "When I look at you, I see his eyes, his…" She pointed to her. "Yes, looking at you, I see the eyes that haunted me for a long time. I didn't think I'd ever be okay, ever be normal. As my waist-line grew, I drowned myself in drugs, whatever it was, to get the image out.

"I'm sorry for what happened to you, but I can't do a happily ever after, because you're a reminder of one of the worst times in my life. You're the child of a monster, and just seeing your face reminds me of him. I'm sorry that sounds cruel, but you showed up here and wanted the truth, the ugly truth. This is it, no sugar-coating it."

The way Carly stared at her, Billy Jo believed her hate was very real. She knew now that what Mark had said was true. Sometimes not knowing was better, and now she couldn't unhear it. She truly understood now that this woman had likely been trying to kill her, a memory of something so horrible.

"I guess now it makes sense why you didn't want me, to see me, to know me," Billy Jo said. "You really do hate me." She heard her voice catch before she felt it in her chest, the ache, the desperation. She wasn't sure Carly would answer her, as she had started to leave, her hand on the curtain.

"I'm sorry, but I can't do this," she said. "I beg you to leave me be, leave me alone, leave my family alone. As irrational as it sounds, I can tell myself over and over that you were innocent, that you were just the result of a horrible, evil act, but I can't change how I feel. To me, you are him, a reminder. Even saying it, it doesn't sound rational, but it's how I feel."

"So did you ever tell him?"

Carly glanced back to her again as she dropped her hand from the curtain. "No, I didn't tell him, even though he was very much there in my life, my father's life. I swear, it was as if he knew what he'd done, and he'd show up and do business with my dad as if to see his trophy. The brothel you were born in was his. He and my father arranged it. I was too strung out. I honestly didn't know what had happened to you. I hoped you were dead. When I was dropped off and locked in a facility for addicts, my father said it had been handled. I never spoke of you or what happened. Again, I'm sorry."

When she pulled back the curtain, Mark was there. He stepped over to the bed, and Carly dragged her gaze over to him as if he were easier to look at.

"I'm sorry, but I can't do this," she said. "I'm sorry you were hurt, but it wasn't me. Please leave me alone. I have a family…"

"They're my sisters," Billy Jo said. She could feel Mark hovering. Did he have any idea of how vile she was? Now at least she had an idea of why she'd felt such loathing for herself while growing up.

Carly just shook her head. Her gaze lingered beyond the curtain, to where Jim Jackson was outside, talking with the chief. So he really knew who she was. "No. I wish you a good life, but that's it," she said. Then she walked out.

Billy Jo felt as if someone had rammed a fist into her stomach. She refused to look at Mark, feeling her eyes burn. "Did you hear her?" she said. There was something about the idea of anyone knowing that she just couldn't handle right now. She couldn't look his way. She was afraid of what she'd see there, what he knew.

"Yeah," he said. "Jim explained some, but I was standing just outside the curtain. How about we get out of here?"

She forced herself to nod, but she could feel she was going to lose it. She fisted a hand to her forehead to hide the tears she never cried, and a sloppy, noisy sob escaped. She felt his hand on her shoulder as she kept her head turned away and struggled to pull it together.

He said nothing but handed a tissue to her.

"Well, you were right about one thing," she said. She blew her nose and dragged the tissue across the tears stinging her face.

"And what was that?"

She sniffed again. "That sometimes it's better not knowing, and once you do, you can't un-ring that bell. I thought nothing could be worse than what I already knew."

This time, she did look up at him, but all he did was shake his head, press his hand to her arm, and gesture to the open curtain. She had expected him to say, "I told you so," but he wasn't that much of an asshole.

The secret she'd learned was something she wished Carly had taken to her grave.

"Let's go," he said.

$$\overline{}$$

Chapter 17

$$\overline{}$$

She was sleeping on his bed, the dog beside her.

Mark jumped on his phone as soon as it rang.

"Mark, it's the chief here. Listen, we found him. It had nothing to do with Carly and Jim. It turned out to be a mechanic, a man by the name of Scott Floyd. Seems his kids were yanked from him, put in foster care, and he blamed her. He was trying to scare her. You should know, too, that he had been watching her."

Mark turned to see Billy Jo standing in the doorway. Evidently, she'd heard his phone ring.

He didn't know what to say to her to make this better. He'd seen the haunted look in her eyes after what Carly had said to her. She was a cruel woman, in his mind. He'd stood there outside that curtain, at a loss, hearing what she said and knowing his words would do nothing.

"Do you mean aside from the photos?"

She gestured to the phone. He was leaning against the countertop, waiting for the coffee to finish brewing. He only nodded and shrugged.

"Yes," the chief said. "We tracked the phone. He says

he bought it from a guy on the island—not Russ, though, to be clear. Carmen found another photo of Ms. McCabe on the phone. He'd been watching her sleep. He'd been following her for a few weeks, by the looks of it. He already admitted to sabotaging her vehicle, so he's looking at a whole host of charges, but it's safe to say she should sleep better now, knowing it wasn't the Jacksons. Like I told you before, they're good people."

Mark only nodded, knowing that in handing him a solved case, the chief was protecting his friends. "Well, thanks for letting me know. I'll tell her," he said, then hung up.

He rested his phone on the butcher block counter and took another second to pull in a breath. The chief protected his island, but it was becoming more apparent now that Chief Shepard played chess better than anyone, as if he'd created the game. He looked back over to Billy Jo, taking in how beat-up she appeared.

"How's your headache?" he said.

She shrugged. He was pretty sure that had been an excuse she gave to be left alone. "Better," she said, then nodded to his phone. "Who was that?"

He reached for the coffeepot and filled a mug. "The chief, with an update. You want coffee?"

She shook her head. "No, just water."

He turned on the tap, filled a glass, and held it out to her. "They caught the guy who sent you those photos. He said he bought the phone from someone on the island. He also confessed to tampering with your car. You remember a man named Scott Floyd?"

She sipped on the water, her brow furrowed. "Yeah. I pulled his two little girls. I was actually on my way to their foster home before the accident. It was one of my stops. Did he do this? Why?"

He dumped some sugar straight from the jar into his coffee. He didn't see a clean spoon, so he reached for a fork in the dish drain and used that to stir. "Upset with you, apparently, for taking his girls. He confessed."

According to the chief, anyway. Mark wondered who was doing up the final report and what it would say. There was just something about authority that he'd always had trouble with. Maybe that was why he couldn't shake the feeling of yet again having smoke and mirrors thrown up in front of him.

"The chief has him caught and talking, so it really had nothing to do with the Jacksons," he said. Too easy, how this had suddenly been tied up once the chief got involved, but that wasn't something Billy Jo needed to hear.

She nodded and lowered her gaze into her water.

"You want to talk about it?" he said. He didn't know how he'd feel, if he were her. He was still trying to wrap his head around what Carly had said, how she felt about Billy Jo. He didn't get it. She'd been just a baby. None of that had been her fault.

"So the Jacksons are off the hook," Billy Jo said. "That should bring me some comfort, but instead there's an angry father who wants to hurt me for protecting his girls. Didn't see that one coming."

He figured that was her way of not answering. "You know how I came to be here on this island?" he said.

What the hell was he doing? He never shared this with anyone.

He wasn't sure if that was a smile he saw from her as she strode over to the worn and very old leather sectional that had come with this cottage. She sat down and pulled her bare feet up on the sofa, curling them beside her, then lifted her glass of water again.

"No, Mark, I have no idea."

He could still hear the edge of anger in her tone, but he was at a loss for what to say to someone whose world had completely crumbled. He made no motion to move as he lifted his coffee and took a swallow, feeling the sweetness he needed in the afternoon.

"We all have someone or something that shapes us into who we are. Mine was a young man by the name of Del Brooks. When you hear about something happening, you ask yourself how many people would make the hard choice to speak up and do the right thing, especially knowing it would be the end of their job or way of life. Many say they would do the right thing, but when it comes right down to it, you'll be able to count them on one hand."

She was staring at him, her expression unreadable. She took a swallow. "Is this where you tell me you understand my situation? Because, Mark, I'm really not in the mood. I don't do the commiseration thing."

"Look, Billy Jo, I understand well how upset you are, and maybe I'm a little pissed for you, too. It's not shared misery or whatever you want to call it. It's just that I was raised by two parents who loved each other very much, who loved me and my brothers and taught us that there's no room for being a liar, a cheat, dishonest. Your word is everything, and so is standing up for what you believe in. You can't turn away or take the easy way out, because it could end up costing you."

This time, she was looking his way, but her expression made him wonder if she'd really heard what he was saying. "Sounds like you did something," she said.

He didn't pull his gaze. "When I first joined the police force back where I grew up, in Snohomish County, I was a deputy. One of the things they taught me was that we protect our own. A cop always has another cop's back. It's a culture, a long-standing code. Some of the situations you go into, you could very well end up dead if the cop you're with doesn't have your back. Trust runs very deep. But what do you do when you witness one of your fellow teammates, a cop, doing something wrong?"

She was tapping her glass. "Sounds to me like you're talking about police culture, the blue wall. Did you do something, speak out about something you shouldn't have? I'm very well aware of that backlash that happens if you do. So tell me, Mark: Something happened, and you didn't remain silent. Am I right?" She was smart, too.

"I was raised better," he said. "I knew there would never be backup again when I walked through a door. At the worst, I could walk into a setup and end up dead. Had I been warned? Yeah. They gave me the talk about being on the same team, and if someone on the team messes up, you stay silent. You hear whispers about officers in other places running areas like their own private mafia kingdoms, collecting money, meting out consequences for those who don't pay. Some go to jail for crimes they haven't committed, some are beaten, some are murdered. Left unchecked, they're rogue officers, allowed to operate with impunity.

"You're taught to never, ever go against a fellow officer, no matter what you believe the truth is. Whatever that officer puts in a report is the truth, no matter what, so help you God. So one day, when I happened to witness what I'll call a shakedown, I told the deputy I worked under, absolutely positive that he'd do something or pat me on the back for uncovering something that was going on under the county's nose. But instead, he pulled me aside and said he didn't want to hear about it. I was told to forget it for my own good and keep my mouth shut.

"Did that stop me? Hell, no. Because I remembered well what my parents had taught me, to never give up. So I went to the county sheriff only to discover that the code of silence is powerful, and it prevents the truth from being heard. I started keeping a journal with names, dates, false arrests, planted evidence. One day, a young man was pulled over in a pickup at one of the farms just at the edge of town. I arrived on the scene, and two other deputies were already there. The young man was on the ground, cuffed, bleeding. He died en route to the hospital. They said he was a drifter, stealing, trying to break in, and the deputies had been answering a call. It was clear they were still getting their story straight, and when I searched the truck, there was no evidence of a robbery.

"In fact, it turned out the young man worked there at the farm as a hired hand, and their story didn't explain the blood on his face, as if he'd taken a beating. They said he'd come at them, refused to co-operate, tried to attack one of the deputies. No one wanted to admit that the young man hadn't done anything. No official call had come in. The man had already been cuffed when I got there. Of course, they were lying, but the official report painted that young man as a thug who'd attacked the officers, saying he had a gun, and they'd found stolen items on him from the owner of the property."

He still wondered what would have happened if he'd just gotten back in his car and left when he'd been told to.

"What did you do, Mark?"

He shrugged, thinking of the file he'd taken to the Feds and the resulting investigation that had come down on the department. They had circled the wagons, and the only one out of a job had been him.

"Whistleblowers are very unpopular," he said. "Next I knew, I was denied access to the locker room and the bathroom, told to piss outside with the rest of the rats. The second I didn't back up their lies and look the other way, I was actively hated by every cop in three counties. The day the sheriff called me into his office and asked for my badge, he said he was doing it for my own good, because the way things were going, he'd be on my parents' doorstep, hat in hand, and I'd be in a pine box. Were the reasons to fire me justified?"

He shook his head. "Suddenly, complaints started coming in about me from fictional complainants, nothing I could fight. I was forced out of a job I was really good at. I was hated and unprotected. Then odd things started happening. I'd come out of the store to find my tires slashed, and no one had seen anything. Then one of my dad's horses was poisoned. One of my nieces found a letter in her backpack from school with my name on it. That was how easy it was to get to me through my family. The message was received. I knew I had to leave town. But being a cop is what I'm good at. I had two options. Either this job or Alaska. I knew what would happen in Alaska, so the choice was easy." He could see he had her full attention.

She nodded. "You know, Mark, that was really depressing. You were trying to cheer me up, so I have to say, your bedside manner needs some work."

The dog came waddling out, tail wagging, and jumped on the sofa beside her. She gave him a pet.

Just then, there was a knock at the front door. He took in Sybil through the glass. She saw him and waved, giving him that smile she had just for him, and when he lifted a hand, she took that as her cue to come in.

"Hey, Mark," she said. "Thought I'd drop by and see if you were up to some dinner, drinks, fun."

He realized she was carrying a bag, likely groceries, not something he'd expected.

She managed to take a few more steps before spotting

Billy Jo on the sofa. "Oh, sorry! I didn't know you had company."

"Hey." Billy Jo lifted her hand.

"Yeah, probably not tonight," Mark said. "I have Billy Jo here, as you can see. You two have met, right? Billy Jo, this is Sybil."

Billy Jo looked over to him and then to Sybil, who was standing in the middle of the room, still exuding the same friendliness she always did.

"Coffeehouse, right?" Sybil said. "I saw you there with Mark the other day. You know, I picked up plenty of food. Why don't I make dinner for all of us?"

Billy Jo lifted a brow. "Well, as you said, Mark, everything is okay on the home front for me now, so why don't you just drop me off there, and then you and Sybil can do whatever you do?"

"Pretty sure the doctor said to keep an eye on you tonight," he replied. "Sorry, Sybil. Billy Jo was in an accident today. How about a rain check?"

She only shrugged, glancing down to the bag she was holding. "Sure, of course," she said. Then she strode over to him, rested her hand on his chest, and rose up on her tiptoes. She pressed a kiss to his lips, then threw him a sassy smile before turning to leave, and she lifted her hand in a wave as she stepped out.

Mark just stood there, wondering what the hell had just happened.

"Didn't know you had a girlfriend," Billy Jo said.

"I don't," he replied. "I told you before that me and relationships don't work."

"Hmm," she said, then nodded. "Whatever you say, Mark. But, nevertheless, girls don't think the same way as guys. Something may not be a relationship for you, but to a girl, it just hasn't manifested into one yet."

He lifted his gaze to the closed door before looking back at the woman in his house, whom he'd bared his secrets to. "So, since you're up and I won't be having any of that dinner Sybil planned to make, what do you say to takeout? You want pizza, burgers, or fish and chips?"

At least that was one way to shut down any talk of Sybil and her attempt at marking a territory that, in his mind, no one would claim.

"How about we pick up a pizza on the way to my place?" she said. "Although this has been fun, I still have a cat at home, and since Scott Floyd is now in jail, I'd like to have a bath, change, and be in my own bed." Billy Jo gave the dog another pat and stood up, then hesitated. "But, in case I didn't say it, good on you for doing the right thing."

Chapter 18

Billy Jo wondered about that hollowness in the pit of her stomach. It had filled her chest, leaving her feeling tired and questioning every one of her choices, all because a woman who should have loved her hated her.

How could someone have that kind of power over her?

That was the one question that ran through her mind as she sat in silence after telling Mark to go. She took in the cold pizza and the wine that was calling her, but instead she yanked open the fridge and pulled out a jug of orange juice, then poured a glass before dialing her phone.

She wanted some alone time. She took in Harley nestled on the chair by the window, curling up as the sun was beginning to set.

"Chase McCabe."

Her dad's voice on the phone grounded her. Just hearing it had tears burning her eyes.

"Hi, Dad," was all she got out. She lifted the glass and took a swallow.

"Hey, sweetheart. How are you doing? Is everything all right?"

Of course, that was his go-to question. She fisted her hand, looking up at the ceiling, the pine she loved, willing herself to pull it together. "Yeah, everything's fine. Sorry, just wanted to call and hear your voice."

It would be so easy to tell him, but then he'd be in his car with her mom, on the next ferry over, to fix whatever he could of the situation in the only way he knew how.

"Is something wrong? What happened?" he said. She had all his attention.

"Why does something have to be wrong?" she replied. "Can't I just call to talk, to see how you and Mom are?" She wasn't sure what she heard in the background, but she knew when her dad was really listening to everything she was saying.

"Absolutely, kiddo, but you don't. Getting anything from you is like pulling teeth. The only time I know something is bothering you is when I can see it. You hold on to everything, always have. So come on, what is it? Did something happen with your job? Your mom and I can be over there in—"

"Dad, stop, seriously. Don't come over. I just wanted to hear your voice. Okay, maybe something happened. I got in an accident—but I'm fine. just a little stiff and sore. I have a couple stitches. I totaled my car. The wheel fell off, and I ended up in the ditch."

There was silence on the other end. She knew that was enough that he'd stop asking, enough to throw him off from knowing everything, because she never wanted him to know she'd found Carly

"But you're okay?" he said. "You don't sound like it. Maybe we should come out, or perhaps it's time for you to come home to visit. We expect you here for Thanksgiving and Christmas, but I think sooner would be better. Your mom was going to call you and remind you to come home, but now you've totaled your car, so you need a new one. You called the insurance company? Better yet, I'll take care of it and get you something decent to drive."

There was something about talking to her dad. It was the reminder she needed that she was wanted, and the way her dad stepped in to organize her life, tell her what to do, try to fix everything for her, was welcome right now, even though she struggled against telling him she could handle it all.

"You don't have to get me a car, Dad," she said. "I can get my own. And that wasn't why I called. I just wanted to say thank you."

There was silence for a second. "Thank you for what, Billy Jo?"

She made herself pull in a breath as a tear slid down her cheek. She was glad her parents weren't there to see it.

"For…?" her dad started.

"For walking into that gas station that day, for not giving up on me."

For wanting me.

"Sounds like you were really rattled in that accident," he said. "You sure you don't want us to come out?"

She was shaking her head as another tear slipped out, and a smile touched her lips. "No, no, Dad, it's fine. I'm okay. I just wanted to hear your voice. Tell Mom I'll call her tomorrow. I love you both."

"Now I know something is really wrong, because you've never once said 'I love you.' But whatever it is that's happened, I'm just glad you know that your mom and I love you very much. And about your car…"

She waited. She knew her dad just couldn't help himself from finding a way to take over her life and fix something, anything. When he didn't say anything more, she said, "Dad, again, I can get my own car. I just wanted to call and hear your voice."

"Okay, but do call your mom tomorrow. And, Billy Jo…" He hesitated.

"Yeah, Dad?"

"You know if there's ever anything, you can talk to me," he said. Now she wondered if he had an idea of what had happened.

"I know," she replied. "Goodnight, Dad."

Then she hung up and took a second before resting her phone on the counter and pulling her hands over her face.

As she walked over to the door, she realized someone was on the balcony. She pulled open the door to face Mark, who was leaning on the railing. He looked back at her.

"Uh, what are you doing here?" she said. She was in her comfy pajamas, and she pulled her arms across her chest, taking in his jean jacket and the way he lingered there. "I told you to go, that I was fine."

She didn't know what to make of the way he was looking at her as he nodded and said, "Sure, but I didn't say I was going to listen. Twenty-four hours is what I heard from the doctor."

"So you're out here, loitering on my porch, because of what the doctor said?" She knew it had come out rather sharply.

"Not the only reason," he replied. He glanced out into the yard and then back to her. "Another is because I care."

It took her a second to realize what he'd said. "Fine," she finally replied, "but I'm going to bed. Keep the TV low so I don't hear it. And I can't swear the cat won't bother you."

Mark followed her back into her apartment and closed

the door, and she took a second to really see him, wondering how it was that the one guy she hadn't expected to like was there, showing her this kind of support.

"So you're really giving up a night with the coffeehouse girl for me?" she said.

He shrugged, then lifted the pizza box and reached for a cold slice. "Hey, friends don't abandon friends when they're down and out."

"I'm not thanking you again," she said. "There's a limit on the number of times I say it in a night."

He let out a laugh and took a bite. "Duly noted. Goodnight, Billy Jo."

The way his blue eyes lingered, she knew he'd never embarrass her with what he'd heard, what Carly had told her.

"Goodnight, Mark," she said. *And thank you.*

What happens when you stumble across a case that should never have been closed?

Detective Mark Friessen uncovers a disturbing mystery: A little girl was taken, but when evidence disappeared, the case was closed.

While cleaning out closed cases, Mark discovers a file on a missing toddler, Gabriele Martin. After reading the two pages within, he realizes evidence is missing. The only interviews, by the detective who previously had Mark's job, was conducted with a bitter ex-wife and a former business partner, both of whom pointed at the father.

It appears to have been an open and shut case. The father took Gabriele in retaliation for a bitter custody dispute with her mother, and then he killed her. Although no body was found, the father was charged and convicted, and the case was closed.

However, an old woman the town has dubbed Crazy Carla disagrees. She says she saw everything, and she contradicts the investigating detective's notes, yet the local cops pursued only one lead, the father.

As Mark secretly delves into the closed case and realizes that nothing adds up, he reaches out to social worker Billy Jo McCabe. Did social services receive any suspicious reports about the girl or her parents? What Billy Jo soon discovers is a family of secrets, a volatile marriage, and a forbidden relationship—and the mystery of the missing girl, whose body has never been found, becomes a case that should never have been closed.

The Cold Case
CHAPTER 1

The feeling of being unprotected was one he knew well, a feeling no one should have to live with. Mark wondered when his instincts had become so deeply embedded, the warning that sent the hair on the back of his neck standing up whenever anything was off.

It was a feeling that just wouldn't fade.

Mark could never be vulnerable, and though he would never be willing to admit to his weaknesses, he didn't take kindly to the familiar sense of unease. After his fellow officers suddenly turned on him, everything he did had gone under a microscope, with problems coming at him in a way he couldn't have explained reasonably.

That had been a painful lesson that he was the only person he could count on.

Maybe it was why his lone-wolf mentality had become so deeply entrenched.

He took in Gail's empty desk, aware that it had been a few days since he'd seen her, and listened to the chief on the phone in his office.

"What are you doing?" Carmen said, suddenly

standing in front of his desk in her light brown deputy uniform, her dark hair pulled back as it always was.

She never smiled.

"I'm on phone duty," he replied, just staring at the phone on his desk, which hadn't rung in a while. He glanced back over to the chief in his office, who was leaning back in his chair. Whomever he was talking to, Mark didn't have a clue.

"So you're planning on just sitting there?" Carmen said, holding a stack of files. She could be quite direct.

"I'm doing as I'm told. Chief said watch the phones, so here I am." He gestured toward the chief's office, not missing the twist of her lips and something else in her eyes before she nodded.

Okay, maybe there was some humor buried deep there —at his expense.

"I'm sure he didn't mean for you to just sit there and stare into space. So come on, give me a hand. There is such a thing as multitasking. Pick up the portable phone and carry it with you. See how easy that is?" She didn't wait for him to follow.

Mark couldn't shake the feeling that the chief had been keeping an especially close eye on him as of late, putting him on what was beginning to feel like a very short leash.

"So what are you doing, anyway?" he asked, grabbing the portable phone and following her through the open door into the back, then down the stairs, old and creaky, to the basement, which was a place he didn't go often. The shelves there appeared dusty.

"Cleaning out files," she said. "We have to make room for cases. Some of these go back years."

Boxes were stacked high on the shelves, labeled with black ink handwriting on the front. Carmen had a box out on the floor now and was shoving the files she had held inside.

"What is all this?" He gestured toward her.

Carmen didn't look up from where she squatted. "All the case files. The current closed ones are in the first row. Gail is usually down here, moving the closed files. Those four sets over there are all the cases that were never solved."

He took in the shelves she gestured to, seeing the sheer number of boxes, and wondered whether he'd heard right. Why didn't he know this? "Are you saying more than half the files down here are unsolved?"

She stood up and slid the box back on the shelf. "I'd say a little more, but that's why you're helping me. Seems some of the cases are mixed up, some cold and unsolved in with the closed and solved. The chief also wants to make room by pulling out everything more than ten years old." The way Carmen talked was so matter of fact at times.

"Excuse me? Pulled out and put where?"

She lifted her gaze to him. Even though Carmen was hard to read, something about the way she'd said it had him pausing.

"Someplace to make room, as the chief said. Once a case is that old, the probability of it ever being solved reverts to just about zero. You know the stats. With us being an island with limited resources, all these old case files are just collecting dust." She tapped the box.

It had him looking at each one, and he felt that off feeling again. Something had happened to someone in each of those files, and he had the sense that justice hadn't been served. "Are you talking about destroying the files? You realize you can't do that."

Carmen pulled a box out and shoved it at his chest,

forcing him to take it. "You really do love to stir things up," she said, and he wasn't sure she was teasing.

He set the box down on a side table. "Carmen, laws are in place for exactly this reason…"

"Who said anything about destroying files? The chief just said they're to be moved out. We need the room. So go through the box, make sure everything is filed correctly and closed, and then mark the file with your initials to say you checked it. The year is marked on the box. Anything older than ten years is to be stacked by the stairs. The chief is having them picked up."

She didn't look his way. He realized Carmen seemed to understand the underbelly of this island better than anyone, how the law seemed to be implemented. She was rifling through a box, and he couldn't help but wonder what she was looking for.

"Picked up by who?" he said. "Or should I not ask? There are supposed to be procedures in place for safe-keeping—you know, evidence you don't want tampered with. You can't exactly have this getting out to the public."

She hesitated but didn't look up. Mark was suddenly more aware of the files he'd closed and tossed on a cabinet by Gail's desk. That was the first thing she had told him about how to handle a case file. She had always put the files away, and he'd never considered for a moment where they went after that.

Carmen didn't appear to be listening.

"You know," Mark said, "it's not lost on me that you won't elaborate on this. So tell me, are the files being moved to storage someplace? Where? For an island this size, there're a lot of unsolved cases going back years."

Carmen was now squatted down at the end of a row of shelves, and he could hear her rustling. Again, she didn't answer.

"Hey, what are you doing?" he said.

She appeared around the corner, holding another box, and he had to remind himself that she had never felt the need to fill any kind of uncomfortable silence. He thought she did it purposely.

"You really do talk too much sometimes," she said. "Here's a thought: Sometimes you may not want answers to the questions you ask. Just have a look through this one, too." She dumped another box beside him.

He took in the unlabeled front. Why did it seem Carmen knew something he didn't? He found himself looking over to her. He wasn't sure whether she hadn't heard his question or just didn't want to answer, but the latter seemed more and more likely.

He opened the box, hearing footsteps squeaking above his head on the floor upstairs in the old building. After taking in the thick files, he pulled one out that was thin, with not much to it, labeled *Martin*. There were only two pages inside, and he flipped them over and took in the file again. It had been closed, apparently an easy case.

"Carmen, this one is dated four years ago, and there're only a couple pages in here. It's a missing toddler, a kid…"

He was reading the report, by a Detective Singer, open and shut. His stomach knotted with a sick feeling at the knowledge that a little kid had been killed, but where were the crime scene photos? It seemed a lot of details were missing. His brow furrowed as he closed up the file and rummaged through the others.

He pulled out another thick one, listening to the silence. When he glanced up, Carmen was standing by the stairs, and he wasn't sure what to make of the way she was watching him. He gestured toward the thin file. "Were you here four years ago? You know about this case? Then there's this Detective Singer."

Carmen walked over to him and took in the file, looking over his arm.

"There has to be something missing, another file," he said, lifting each one out. He didn't know why this bothered him, sloppy filing, sloppy work.

"I doubt it," was all she said, flipping through the two sheets. When she closed the file, her expression was matter of fact again.

Mark pulled out yet another file from the box, seeing a different case on each one.

"Paperwork wasn't really the detective's forte," Carmen said. "He always seemed to keep everything up here." She tapped her head, and it took him a second to realize she was serious.

"Really? You're messing with me. That file has no crime scene photos. Where's the body, a confession, a few notes?" He took the file from Carmen, who seemed more than happy to let him have it. One page was labeled *Interview*, and a note at the top said *Open and shut*. "Come on. You have to give me something, here. Who was this Detective Singer, anyway?"

She shot him a heavy stare, and he wasn't sure what was behind it.

"Who is this? There's a note in here about a Crazy Carla." He took in the name underlined in red. "So are these the kinds of files we're packing up and moving out of here? This is sloppy. How many more are like this?" He found himself reaching for another file, seeing Detective Singer's name in there. Again, the paperwork was lacking, but all Carmen did was shrug. "I know you worked with him. Come on, Carmen, seriously, what is this?"

"Look, Detective Singer was here before me—long before me, if you get my drift. I was just lucky he didn't train me. The chief did. So go through the files there and have a look. Make sure nothing's missing."

He couldn't pull his gaze from her, even when the chief called from upstairs, "Mark!"

Carmen pulled in a breath and pressed her lips together, glancing back to the stairs.

"Downstairs," Mark called. He heard footsteps, and the chief appeared in the doorway, looking down.

"Have to make a run out," the chief said. "What are you doing down there?"

He realized Carmen had stepped away. He made himself take a step over to the stairs and looked up, still holding the file. "Giving Carmen a hand with all these old files," he said. He didn't know why he didn't bother elaborating.

The chief only nodded. "Fine, shouldn't take long. Just stack them and leave them. Gail's on her way in, and then you can get out there and make rounds," he said. Then he just stood there for a second, and Mark wondered what was on his mind. The chief just inclined his head and walked away.

Odd. He had been sure the chief was about to say something. He listened to the footsteps and the door closing. When he turned back, there was Carmen with an odd look on her face.

"You know, sometimes when a case has been mishandled, you can't say anything if it's not yours," she said, pulling her arms across her chest and nodding at the file he was still holding.

He wondered if that was a question. "Sure," he said. "That's one of the reasons I work out here. So what are you getting at?"

Her eyes were brown. She didn't look away. "That

feeling you have when something isn't right… Not all cops have it. You know what I mean?"

He knew. It was that feeling he had, which seemed to always be there.

"Let me ask you this, Carmen. Did you hand me this box with this file because you know something was mishandled?"

She blinked and stepped back, then looked away just as he heard the door upstairs. "You know, why don't I do rounds for you?" she said. "Sometimes it feels as if the walls are closing in on me here."

There it was, her unwillingness to answer. Another complex woman who seemed to live and breathe secrets.

About the Author

"Lorhainne Eckhart is one of my go to authors when I want a guaranteed good book. So many twists and turns, but also so much love and such a strong sense of family."

(Lora W., Reviewer)

New York Times & USA Today bestseller Lorhainne Eckhart is best known for her writing Raw Relatable Real Romances, where "Morals and family are running themes. Danger, romance, and a drive to do what is right will see you glued to the page." As one fan calls her, she is the "Queen of the family saga." (aherman) writing "the ups and downs of what goes on within a family but also with some suspense, angst and of course a bit of romance thrown in for good measure." Follow Lorhainne on Bookbub to receive alerts on New Releases and Sales and join her mailing list at LorhainneEckhart.com for her Monday Blog, books news, giveaways and FREE reads. With over 120 books, audiobooks, and multiple series published and available at all retailers now translated into six languages. She is a multiple recipient of the Readers' Favorite Award for Suspense and Romance, and lives in the Pacific Northwest on an island, is the mother of three, her oldest has autism and she is an advocate for never giving up on your dreams.

"Lorhainne Eckhart has this uncanny way of just hitting the spot every time with her books."

(Caroline L., Reviewer)

The O'Connells: *The O'Connells of Livingston, Montana are not your typical family. A riveting collection of stories surrounding the ups and downs of what goes on within a family but also with some suspense, angst and of course a bit of romance thrown in for good measure "I thought I loved the Friessens, but I absolutely adore the O'Connell's. Each and every book has totally different genres of stories but the one thing in common is how she is able to wrap it around the family which is the heart of each story." (C. Logue)*

The Friessens: *An emotional big family romance series, the Friessen family siblings find their relationships tested, lay their hearts on the line, and discover lasting love! "Lorhainne Eckhart is one of my go to authors when I want a guaranteed good book. So many twists and turns, but also so much love and such a strong sense of family." (Lora W., Reviewer)*

The Parker Sisters: *The Parker Sisters are a close-knit family, and like any other family they have their ups and downs. "Eckhart has crafted another intense family drama…The character development is outstanding, and the emotional investment is high…" (Aherman, Reviewer)*

The McCabe Brothers: *Join the five McCabe siblings on their journeys to the dark and dangerous side of love! An intense, exhilarating collection of romantic thrillers you won't want to miss. — "Eckhart has a new series that is definitely worth the read. The queen of the family saga started this series with a spin-off of her wildly successful Friessen series." From a Readers' Favorite award— winning author and "queen of the family saga" (Aherman)*

Billy Jo McCabe Mystery: *The social worker and the cop, an unlikely couple drawn together on a small, secluded Pacific Northwest island where nothing is as it seems. Protecting the innocent comes at a cost, and what seems to be a sleepy, quiet town is anything but.*

Lorhainne loves to hear from her readers! You can connect with me at:
www.LorhainneEckhart.com
lorhainneeckhart.le@gmail.com

facebook.com/AuthorLorhainneEckhart

twitter.com/LEckhart

instagram.com/lorhainneeckhart

bookbub.com/profile/lorhainne-eckhart

pinterest.com/lorhainneeckhart

Also by Lorhainne Eckhart

The Outsider Series
The Forgotten Child (Brad and Emily)
A Baby and a Wedding *(An Outsider Series Short)*
Fallen Hero (Andy, Jed, and Diana)
The Search *(An Outsider Series Short)*
The Awakening (Andy and Laura)
Secrets (Jed and Diana)
Runaway (Andy and Laura)
Overdue *(An Outsider Series Short)*
The Unexpected Storm (Neil and Candy)
The Wedding (Neil and Candy)

The Friessens: A New Beginning
The Deadline (Andy and Laura)
The Price to Love (Neil and Candy)
A Different Kind of Love (Brad and Emily)
A Vow of Love, A Friessen Family Christmas

The Friessens
The Reunion
The Bloodline (Andy & Laura)
The Promise (Diana & Jed)
The Business Plan (Neil & Candy)
The Decision (Brad & Emily)
First Love (Katy)
Family First
Leave the Light On
In the Moment

In the Family
In the Silence
In the Charm
Unexpected Consequences
It Was Always You
The First Time I Saw You
Welcome to My Arms
Welcome to Boston
I'll Always Love You
Ground Rules
A Reason to Breathe
You Are My Everything
Anything For You
The Homecoming
Stay Away From My Daughter
The Bad Boy
A Place of Our Own
The Visitor
All About Devon
Long Past Dawn
How to Heal a Heart
Keep Me In Your Heart

The O'Connells
The Neighbor
The Third Call
The Secret Husband
The Quiet Day
The Commitment
The Missing Father
The Hometown Hero
Justice
The Family Secret

The Fallen O'Connell
The Return of the O'Connells
And The She Was Gone
The Stalker
The O'Connell Family Christmas
The Girl Next Door

The McCabe Brothers
Don't Stop Me (Vic)
Don't Catch Me (Chase)
Don't Run From Me (Aaron)
Don't Hide From Me (Luc)
Don't Leave Me (Claudia)
Out of Time

A Billy Jo McCabe Mystery
Nothing As it Seems
Hiding in Plain Sight
The Cold Case
The Trap
Above the Law

The Wilde Brothers
The One (Joe and Margaret)
The Honeymoon, A Wilde Brothers Short
Friendly Fire (Logan and Julia)
Not Quite Married, A Wilde Brothers Short
A Matter of Trust (Ben and Carrie)
The Reckoning, A Wilde Brothers Christmas
Traded (Jake)
Unforgiven (Samuel)
The Holiday Bride

Married in Montana
His Promise
Love's Promise
A Promise of Forever

The Parker Sisters
Thrill of the Chase
The Dating Game
Play Hard to Get
What We Can't Have
Go Your Own Way
A June Wedding

Kate & Walker
One Night
Edge of Night
Last Night

Walk the Right Road Series
The Choice
Lost and Found
Merkaba
Bounty
Blown Away: The Final Chapter

The Saved Series
Saved
Vanished
Captured

Single Titles
He Came Back
Loving Christine

For my German Readers
Die Außenseiter-Reihe
Der Vergessene Junge
Der Gefallene Held

For my French Readers
L'ENFANT OUBLIÉ